THE KNIFE ACTED
LIKE GLUE IN MY HAND.

No electrostatic force was stronger.
My muscles were paralyzed
from the psychometric power
locked within the small blade.

I'll scream.

The screech deafened me—
but only me.
No one else could have heard
the wail of utter anguish.
Someone was being skinned alive
with this knife.
And I was sharing
the sick triumph of the man
slowly killing him ...

Other Peter Thorne Mysteries by
Robert E. Vardeman
from Avon Books

THE SCREAMING KNIFE

THE
RESONANCE
OF
BLOOD

ROBERT E. VARDEMAN

AVON BOOKS ◆ NEW YORK

THE RESONANCE OF BLOOD is an original publication of Avon Books. This work has never before appeared in book form. This work is a novel. Any similarity to actual persons or events is purely coincidental.

AVON BOOKS
A division of
The Hearst Corporation
1350 Avenue of the Americas
New York, New York 10019

First Avon Books Printing: February 1992

AVON TRADEMARK REG. U.S. PAT. OFF. AND IN OTHER COUNTRIES, MARCA REGISTRADA, HECHO EN U.S.A.

Printed in the U.S.A.

RA   10   9   8   7   6   5   4   3   2   1

For Dennis, the lunatic artist

CHAPTER 1

Everything was going wrong and there was nothing I could do to prevent it. I stopped in the middle of a bit of misdirection to get the audience looking in the wrong place and stared past the bright stage lights. The audience was beginning to drift. One or two coughed and some even yawned, sure signs I was losing their interest. Glancing back toward my assistant, Julianne, gave me part of the reason for the audience's lack of attention.

She was staring offstage and not tending to her part of the trick. If I finished the sleight of hand, I would look ridiculous. Julianne had missed her cue, and only the blind or the terminally gullible couldn't see how the trick was done. Covering her lapse, I spun, my short satin cape swinging wide. Heavy weights in the bottom made it flare just right, allowing me to find the flash paper fastened along one seam.

The sweeping gesture and the bright flare from the paper brought Julianne's attention back to her job. I decided to cut the act short for the night.

I should have finished the vanishing trick, making the three ducks go away and then come back as a small lion cub. I don't enjoy working with animals, but the manager at the Rialto, whose stage I was currently disgracing, insisted on their inclusion in the act. His audiences enjoyed animals, he said. At the moment I wasn't thinking charitable thoughts about the manager's insistence, the animal-loving audience, or my assistant.

Ignoring the lion cub's snarls from the hidden pocket at the back of the small table where the ducks stirred nervously, I spun again and produced a deck of cards. I let them fly into the air with a loud rush. As they sailed toward the audience they turned into a gently cascading shower of brightly colored, light-reflecting confetti. It was a simple enough finish for the act, but it made the first two rows stiffen and flinch in surprise as they saw first the cards and then the soft, glittery dust come down on them.

"Thank you all very much. You've been too kind this evening." I bowed deeply. The applause was lackluster but still more than I had expected. Even the best magician has an off night, though I could hardly believe Houdini had one, or Thurston or even Blackstone. I started to exit when a booming voice stopped me.

"Hey, you can't stop the show. Not yet," came an angry cry from the audience. "You've only been on twenty minutes."

I had learned early in my career that arguing with anyone in the audience is a no-win game. What bothered me the most was that the complaint was valid. I was cheating the paying customers by not giving them the best show possible.

"Do the reading gimmick. I saw you do that once. Do the psychometry thing."

Coldness welled inside me at the suggestion. Like all performers doing a mentalist act, I had worked out a series of code words with my assistant. However, I don't have to depend on anyone to perform this feat. This was no parlor game for me, no simple state illusion. For me psychometry was real and required considerable mental effort. I wasn't sure if I could concentrate enough for a true demonstration. I was too angry at Julianne for missing her cues all night long.

Glancing into the wings, I saw Barry Morgan standing with his arms crossed. The theater manager's barrel chest heaved up and down as he puffed away at his cigarette. With the cloud of smoke rising around him he looked like a demon from hell. Actually, even without the engulfing blue smoke, the set to his rotund body and the way he squinted at me from under the bony ridges where eyebrows had once been made him look like a demon's spawn. He gestured angrily that I should get on with it. A quick look at Julianne told me she wasn't going to be able to pick up on any significant cue. The confused look on her face spoke more clearly than words. She was lost and any attempt to bring her back up to speed for the act would fail.

"Psychometry," I said in a deep voice, trying to stretch the act. "An ancient art and one not performed lightly. I shall require absolute quiet and a few moments to meditate and elevate myself to a higher plane."

A few flourishes gave the impression I was beginning my meditation. The light man picked up on the cue and shifted the color of the lights constantly, dropping first one gel and then another to give me an other-worldly aspect. It was too much to hope that Julianne would be able feed me the word clues needed to fake the act.

I was going to have to touch objects from the audience and sense—merge with—their vibrations. Doing this sapped my energy quickly. I wouldn't be able to do more than two or three objects.

"What do you want me to do?" whispered Julianne.

"Into the audience," I called in a loud voice. "Blindfold me securely and then go forth into the audience and bring me several objects to read."

Julianne looked confused again, not sure what to do since this wasn't supposed to be part of the act. She shrugged and then made her way down the stairs at stage right. The light man followed her with the Fresnel spotlight while he dropped a gobo in front of the ellipsoidal spot's gate and formed a glowing triangle above my head. He started getting into the spirit of the act then. I wanted to give him a raise, a bonus, my firstborn son. He was saving me just as surely as Julianne had been torpedoing me.

New Brigham colors formed in the triangle, changing from medium magenta to fire red and finally settling on a cool Nile blue. By then I looked as composed as possible. Julianne took a large black silk handkerchief and fastened it over my eyes before leaving to get items from the audience.

"I have three objects," Julianne said after a minute's delay. "Are you ready to receive them?"

She remembered some of the code words we had worked on when we had used this act more than a month ago. She had told me she had a key ring with five keys, a pocket knife, and a woman's cheap wristwatch.

"I will not bother with the lady's watch," I said. "It isn't a Rolex." The audience giggled a little at the woman. "It isn't even a Timex. And it is eight minutes slow."

Julianne held up the watch for several nearby spectators in the audience to see. Even with the blindfold, I knew human nature. People would be checking their own watches. This was going better than it had any right to.

"The keys," I said, playing on my small success. "Bring me the key ring with the five keys on it."

This impressed a few more. I was struggling. I'd take all the approval I could get. My assistant handed me the keys. Everything to this point had been strictly showmanship. Now was the time to use my unique gift—or as it usually seems, my curse. I can touch an inanimate object and read the psychic vibrations imprinted on it by its owner, if that imprinting is strong enough.

"A car key, a Ford. A red Ford," I added, feeling a rising tide of tension around me. The woman who owned the car had driven it for years. "Nine years you have owned the car. It . . . it has trouble." I began to struggle with the impressions flooding over me. The car was the most important thing in the woman's life. The other keys carried almost no imprint for me to work. But the car, the damned red Ford.

"It was your father's," I said, seeing a funeral procession and hearing soft crying. I shivered. The psychic perceptions became twisted and ghostlike. "A funeral. You inherited the car from your father."

I dropped the keys to the stage. Sweat beaded on my forehead and stained the blindfold. The fleeting glimpses I'd received into the woman's life had not been worth the strain.

"Is this true?" called out Julianne, picking up when she saw that I wasn't able to continue.

"How did he know?" came a choked voice. "That's all my father left me. But it's not red."

"The car has been repainted," I said without thinking. I rubbed my clammy palms on my thighs. I was sitting cross-legged on a low table and wobbling. From under the corner of the blindfold, I saw that the lighting director was changing the gels again to make it seem as if my mental powers were rippling over my head. The old-style Brighams gave only seventy-five colors, but he must have run through most of them.

When the woman in the audience said, "You're right. It *was* red. How'd you know that?" Her voice was shrill with strain.

"Psychometry can reveal much," I said. I allowed myself a few seconds to collect myself and do a mantra to compose my thoughts and settle my emotions. Licking dried lips, I accepted the pocket knife.

The spotlight hit the object in my hand, going from blue to dazzling white. But I didn't have to look at the knife.

I *saw* it.

I *felt* it.

I *heard* it.

That hurts. Why are you doing this? Stop! Ouch! I don't want you doing that. Stop!

I tried to force it away, to drop it, to distance myself mentally from it. The knife acted as if it were glued to my hand. No electrostatic force was stronger. My muscles were paralyzed from the psychometric power locked within the small blade.

I'll scream.

The screech deafened me—but only me. No one else could have heard the wail of utter anguish before death seized the man. He was being skinned to death with this knife. And I was sharing the sick triumph of the man slowly killing him. Each deft flourish peeled back a small curlicue segment of skin from arm and leg and throat. Blood. It flowed. My hands were drenched.

The knife clattered to the stage as I teetered and almost fell off the table.

"What is your reading?" came Julianne's voice. It sounded as if she had moved to Monterey and was speaking through a long tube. "Tell us of the knife's owner."

"I can't," I said in a voice so low only Julianne heard. Louder, "There is nothing significant to tell about him." I whipped off the blindfold. Standing on shaking legs, I moved to the front of the stage and motioned for the light man to lower the intensity on both the Fresnel and the ellipsoid spotlights. I needed to look into the audience.

"Whose knife was I given? I cannot read anything from it," I lied. "Allow me to return it personally." I scanned the audience but no one moved.

"Julianne? Whose knife was it?"

"It was passed down the fourth row," she said. "I didn't see whose it was." That alone infuriated me. For the stunt to work, she needed to observe carefully and pass along information using seemingly innocuous code words. Julianne hadn't paid any attention to the man giving her the knife.

My eyes darted along that row and focused on the single empty seat. The knife's owner had been here but had gone. There were questions I needed to ask that . . . animal.

"The man seemed to have left." I knelt and picked up the cheap plastic-handled knife with some distaste. Slipping it into my pocket lessened the force of its psychic message. It did nothing to remove the psychic blister it had put on my emotions.

The unholy screams. The agony. The man dying as the murderer killed his victim by inches. It all jumbled together, murderer and murdered. I relived that they both thought and felt in a welter of confusing sensations.

Bleed for me! Go on, bleed! I want to see your blood flowing in rivers, in buckets, in a tidal wave!

"Thank you for your kind attention to my legerdemain." I bowed quickly and almost ran from the stage. Nothing had gone right this evening. If Julianne hadn't missed so many of her cues, I would never have had to resort to psychometry to keep the audience interested.

The penknife. Deadly. It had been used to kill. Slowly.

I rubbed the sweat from my face, barely aware of the sporadic applause from the audience. There was no need for me to worry about a curtain call. The show had not been that good. The one direct hit with the woman's car had rocked her but had passed most of the audience by. The biggest sensation had been the woman's inexpensive watch. Julianne ought to have given all the objects to me using our specific code words to describe them.

I turned to her and braced myself against the back wall, trying to get strength back into my legs. "What happened, Julianne?" I tried to keep from shouting. "You missed your cues repeatedly tonight. If I had finished the last trick, I'd've had three ducks *and* that damned lion cub on the table at the same time."

"I'm sorry, Mr. Thorne. It's just not my night. You know how it is sometimes." She tried to shrug, but I wasn't going to let it go at that. I had been forced into displaying my psychometric powers and I didn't like that one bit.

"Come on back to my dressing room. We're going to have this out." I made as theatrical an exit as I could, but I knew it wouldn't impress Julianne. She had been my assistant for almost four months and was moderately good at her job. I wished now that she had screwed things up earlier in her brief tenure with me so I would have had the motivation to replace her. The truth was, finding a magician's assistant was difficult. My prior assistant had gotten pregnant and left the act.

Julianne was an out-of-work actress who had been recommended by a friend at the Magic Castle down in Los Angeles. I wondered what appropriate revenge I could wreak on him.

Before I got to my dressing room, the theater manager stopped me.

"I want a word with you, Thorne. That was one piss-poor show you put on tonight. What was with you and all that psychic shit? It didn't impress anybody out there, me included. I'm paying you top dollar. I expect more. Hell, even the geeks out in the audience do. There wasn't a one of 'em what believed you really sawed her in half." Morgan jerked his thumb in Julianne's direction.

Considering how poorly many of the tricks had gone, I'd thought the old sawing-a-woman-in-half gimmick had been the most effective in the entire act. I'd added several new twists, including a set of mirrors showing all sides of the box as the buzz saw sliced through Julianne. I was sorry now I hadn't really cut her in two— and offered to put Morgan in the box with her.

"It wasn't my best effort," I admitted. "There are a few bugs I have to work out of the act. Julianne and I were just—"

"Don't care shit for what you're doing. Improve the damned act or you're outta here. Got that?"

I bristled. I wasn't used to such criticism, even if it was as deserved as it was tonight. Watching the balding patch on the man's head as he left mesmerized me. The play of light and shadow turned the spot into the doorway to hell. For a moment, I returned to the hideous world shown me by the knife in my pocket.

"Mr. Thorne, I don't have all night."

Glaring at Julianne, I held the door open and let her precede me into the small dressing room. I walked to the rack, hung up my cape and jacket and put a squawking pigeon that hadn't been used on its perch. Julianne had missed an earlier cue and had left me in the middle of the stage with two other birds. Pulling the third one out would have made me look foolish.

"Tonight's not going to happen again. You can do better. You have done better. Is there a reason you kept missing your cues?"

The woman's expression didn't change. She was in some far-off land where anyone else was a stranger. She hadn't used drugs during the few months we'd worked together, or at least she hadn't seemed to. But sometimes it was difficult to tell. Julianne's thoughts were often elsewhere. Until tonight, though, she had been reasonably responsive on stage.

Having good legs made up for many of her lapses. Stage magic is entirely sleight of hand and misdirection. Having a pretty assistant who can distract the audience during an illusion, even for a split second, is necessary.

"I'm quitting, Mr. Thorne."

"There's no need to do that." She'd turned a good act into a travesty tonight, but that was no reason to quit and really leave me in the lurch.

"Yeah, there is. Me and my boyfriend are going to St. Louis. We've been talking about it for a couple weeks."

"You and Ben?"

"Ben?" Julianne looked confused for a moment. "Him? I haven't been with Benny for almost a month. Longer. No, me and Jon decided San Francisco was too expensive. We can get real good jobs in St. Louis. He's got a friend who runs a construction company on the Illinois side of the city. Jon's a carpenter and he said he could get me a job as secretary or something."

"How much notice are you giving?"

"I'm leaving in the morning. Jon's got the car all packed."

I almost panicked. My mind raced. It would require

real magic to find another assistant before tomorrow's performance. And it would take an act of God to get one who was already trained. A single botched stunt and the audience saw how a trick was done. That ruined the illusion for all time. I remembered my disappointment as an eight-year-old after watching a careless magician perform the Chinese linking rings. I had seen clearly how he did the trick and every time after that, no matter how good the illusionist, I saw the way the rings were held, where the broken ring moved, everything.

The object of stage magic is to tell the audience it's all a trick, then perform so that they think you lied, to make them assume that the trick must really be occurring. They might not believe intellectually but emotionally their minds would continue to work for days trying to figure out how the trick was really done. They had *seen* and seeing was believing. That even brought some back for multiple performances.

That level of expertise requires an adept assistant.

"This is too sudden," I said. My thoughts refused to fall into any coherent order. The lump formed in my pocket by the knife still distracted me. I had to talk to the police. Maybe they knew something about a penknife murder.

"Yeah, real sudden, but Jon's like that. Spontaneous. That's what I like about him better than Benny. I'm real sorry tonight didn't work out, Mr. Thorne."

A new assistant. By tomorrow's performance. How? *Bleed, you son of a bitch!*

I shook and tears formed in the corners of my eyes.

"Hey, don't take it so hard. Look, if it breaks you up so much, dock my salary for tonight. I'll give you a temporary address where you can mail my check."

"Yes, your check." Dazed, I watched as Julianne scribbled on the back of an envelope. Finishing, she started to say something more. She bit her lower lip and swallowed hard. She stared at me as if I were a visitor from another planet, then rushed out of my dressing room. Jon must be waiting for her. This revelation came far too late for me.

I needed another assistant.

Look at the skin as it peels away from your body. You never knew it came off in such pretty geometric patterns, did you, you worthless piece of shit?

I turned to my dressing table and put my head down on my crossed arms. Gathering my wits about me, I tried to settle my mind. Imagining pools of placid blue water, floating on soft white clouds, drifting like an autumn leaf on a gentle breeze—none of the usual methods of relaxation worked.

Reaching into my pocket, I pulled out the offending knife and dropped it on the table as if it had burned me. Its seeming innocence belied the hideous emotional power locked within its metallic lattice.

So many problems. Would they never end? Julianne leaving so unexpectedly threatened my professional reputation. Finding another assistant on such short notice wasn't going to be easy. And the damned knife. Just touching it promised more than a brush with insanity.

"Hey, Mr. Thorne, you got a phone call."

I jerked around and saw a stagehand poking his head through the doorway. He hadn't even bothered to knock. He ducked back when he saw the expression on my face. Killing wasn't something I would ever find easy to do, but at the moment my fear and rage knew few bounds. He had read that and more.

Heaving myself to my feet, I went outside to the pay phone hanging precariously on the stage's back wall. The handset was resting on top of the squat black box. I pressed it to one ear and stuck my index finger in my other ear to shut out the clatter of stagehands moving the scenery. They were setting up for a mid-morning production of some civic group's fund-raising performance of *Our Town*.

"Hello," I said, wondering who would be calling me.

"That you, Peter? You sound strung out. You're not doing any of those new synthetic drugs, are you?"

"What?"

"Ecstasy, Blithe Spirit, Heaven, you know. The designer drugs. The ones cooked up by the chemistry geniuses."

"Hello, Willie," I said, finally recognizing the voice. "What can I do for you?" Willie Worthington was a detective sergeant with the San Francisco Police Department violent crimes unit—his speciality was homicide. He occasionally called on my expertise as a psychometrician to help ferret out clues hidden from normal forensics examinations.

"We got a murder," he said. "I'd consider it a personal favor if you could come down to the Bay and look this one over using your particular, uh, skills."

After all I'd been through tonight, I almost told him what he could do for me as a personal favor. I relented. Even the stubby, well-chewed yellow pencil he used to take notes wouldn't fit that way, no matter how hard he crammed it.

CHAPTER 2

I parked my red BMW just outside the police line. A bored-looking uniformed officer started to motion me away when Worthington bellowed, "He's okay. Let him through, Masataro."

He gave me a once-over and then lifted the yellow plastic strip for me. I pulled my coat collar up against the brisk wind blowing off the Bay. The police line, the Golden Gate Bridge looming over me like a dark vulture, the ponderous mass of Fort Point, all weighed down on me. I wasn't in the best of moods before I came out here. Second by second even that bleak foulness was looking like stark joy.

"Glad you could make it, Peter," the detective said. He had the stub of yellow pencil balanced behind one ear. "Damned place to find a floater. If they make it this far, they usually go on out to sea."

My mood turned darker. A floater. Worthington wanted me to psychometrize something from a body that had been in the Bay for who knows how long. I shuddered as I pictured what the poor bastard must look like. A day or two was bad enough. Fish nibbled at the flesh; sometimes a shark took out huge chunks. Even if the body escaped such ignominy, decay caused gases inside the gut to blow up the abdomen like a kid's toy balloon. I'd heard ambulance drivers trading war stories about finding a floater, touching it, and having it explode like a bomb, sending gore everywhere. They'd thought this was about the funniest thing they'd ever seen since it had happened to a new driver. My imagination is good enough to picture the scene vividly. My stomach started to churn.

"Got any antacid on you?" I asked. Worthington fumbled in his pocket and silently handed me a roll of wintergreen Rolaids.

"Spells relief," I muttered as I gobbled two of them. I palmed a third just in case.

"Damn things don't work for me."

"That's because you don't eat anything but hot dogs. Mystery meat will do you in every time. There's not enough sodium carbonate in the world to put out a gastric acid fire like you must have."

"I can handle the dogs," Worthington grumbled. "It's everything else that wears on me. Hell, Peter, you wouldn't believe the day I've had."

"I don't want to hear it," I said, knowing I would anyway. "I've had one myself."

"Three murders in two days. All tossed in my lap, and me shorthanded. I got two men on administrative leave, I got one who's cracked up and seeing a shrink—and the first two might go the same route. The one was involved in a shooting."

Memory slowly shifted into gear. I had seen the *Chronicle* story a couple days back. "The eleven-year-old kid?" I asked.

"The same. The one cut him down, thinking he was a perp. The damned kid had one of those stupid toy zap guns. Looks and sounds like a laser or something. So anyway, the one guy shoots him by accident and his partner gets his hat shot off by the real perpetrator. Scared the shit out of him."

"The shooter got away, didn't he?"

"Yeah," Worthington said sourly. "And I got two men who might cash it in, each for a different reason. One cuts down a kid and the other has the shit scared out of him. What a mess."

"It's not so easy for me either," I said, feeling almost guilty at my trivial problems.

"Then the floater turns up. Damnation," Worthington went on, not even hearing me. "This isn't the kind of thing that makes you want to rush out and get a good meal."

"You wouldn't know a good meal if it fell on you."

"You've been over when Mary's fixed some of her special meat loaf. You know why I eat what I do. And the doctor's on my case about high cholesterol levels. Hell, when do I have time to eat anything that's decent?"

"You know what they say, Willie. If it tastes good, spit it out."

"Yeah, spit it out." Worthington flipped open his spiral notebook, pulled the pencil from behind his ear, and started scribbling new notes to himself. He had only been talking to fill the silence while he thought about the murder. Now he was putting down whatever new ideas had occurred to him. I let him write. I wished I had something to distract me as I shivered in the cold and dark.

Fort Point had been built during the Civil War and never used; not a shot was ever fired. Somehow the Confederacy had never seen fit to invade San Francisco. During World War II it had been one of a series of coastal defense batteries stretching along the coast from far to the north to south of the Presidio. Not much remained of those sixteen-inch defense guns. The old fort had been renovated as an historical monument for the tourists. The grim brick structure and the heavy iron cannon pointing out to sea were about as appealing as Alcatraz.

A new gust of wet, cold wind whipped off the Bay. I wanted nothing more than to go home and worry. Where was I going to get another assistant before tomorrow's performance? I thought about Barry Morgan and his insistence on using animals. Canceling the act started looking better to me. Some stage magicians had a rapport with birds and cute puppies and small carnivores. I didn't. Taking care of them when I wasn't on-stage was a continual hassle. If I canceled the show, I could take the time to find a good assistant and work up a few flashy and usually well-received escapes. Those were more to my liking, even if one had caused the brain damage that gave me the peculiar psychometric talent.

". . . days," Worthington was saying.

I snapped out of my reverie and tried to piece together everything he'd said.

"Can't be sure, though. Those slugs from the ME's office are taking their sweet time getting out here. It's been damned near two hours. You know how they can be when it's late at night."

"They like their sleep," I mumbled.

"So, what do you think?" Worthington moved away and let me see the corpse.

The antacid tablets didn't work. I puked my guts out.

"Ah, Peter, you should have warned me. Now I've got to mark off the spot where you threw up and tell the forensics guys to ignore it." Worthington scribbled away in his notebook, adding more notes about the condition of the scene.

My stomach refused to settle down. I gobbled the third antacid tablet and let it soak up some of the bile.

"I told you it wasn't pretty," Worthington said. "So?"

"So she's been cut in half," I said. The lower half of a woman's body was bloated from being in the water two or three days, possibly longer. The Bay was especially cold this time of year and might have delayed decay for as long as a week. I wasn't expert in such matters.

Somehow, that was just fine with me.

"I figure she must have come up against a ship's propeller. The cut marks look like a huge blade did her in. She might have been a jumper." Worthington glanced at the black hulk of the Golden Gate Bridge's underside. "We haven't had any reports, though. They've been keeping a good watch for jumpers ever since that senator's kid did herself in last year."

I forced myself to close my eyes. The image refused to die in my brain. It was as if I saw the poor woman's severed torso as clearly as if I stared directly at her. I swallowed my rising gorge and tried to calm myself. The relaxation techniques that had worked only partially for me earlier did a better job now.

"You going to be all right? I don't want you on the walking wounded list, too. The department shrink's got more than she can handle with just my squad."

"I'm all right now. I just wasn't ready for this."

"Who is?" Worthington nibbled at his pencil and put a few more tooth marks into the soft wood. Sometimes I think he is part termite and this is the only sustenance he gets. But I'd seen what he eats for lunch and knew that couldn't be true. The wood might be better for him, but Worthington ate other things.

"There's no way of identifying the body?"

"Can't figure out what it might be. We don't keep footprint records. There aren't any tattoos to track down, and what woman's likely to mention a scar below her waist?"

"I can't psychometrize human flesh. You know that."

"Only personal items. I know. Here. It was an ankle bracelet. That's all there is to go on. Otherwise, Ms. Jane Doe goes into the disgusting but pending file."

"You're not confident of ever getting an ID on her, are you?"

Worthington shook his head. He circled the body—or what remained of it—and stared down. "I've got other irons in the fire, but unless someone reports her missing, there's not a snowball's chance in hell of finding out who she was. Even then . . ." He shrugged.

I understood. If a husband or lover or friend came forward and reported a woman missing, there was almost no chance of getting a positive match. DNA typing goes only so far.

"She might have a distinctive broken leg that didn't mend quite right," I said.

"And she might be Mother Teresa, except she's

probably younger," Worthington said. "We're not sanguine about it unless you can come up with something."

"Do you really want me to?"

"It's going to be a bitch, no matter what, but yeah, I do. I hate having pending files. Somewhere someone's crying over her. It's better to know she's dead than to keep hoping year after year."

I took the plastic bag holding the simple gold anklet. Turning it over and over I studied it to get some idea of the woman's tastes. The anklet was inexpensive, gold-filled rather than gold, and had faint initials engraved. I looked up at Worthington.

"Might be hers," he said. "The initials might also be a boyfriend's. I'm having a computer check done down at Records on all MCs in Missing Persons files."

"She's been in the Bay for a week?"

"Maybe that. It might be long enough for someone to go to Missing Persons and file a report. We're covering that, but it's not too good a bet, Peter. You know that."

"I know the odds," I said.

Cold water dashed restlessly against the nearby stones that prevented this part of the point from washing back into the Bay. The spray distracted me. I needed a few minutes to meditate and settle my mind even more. Getting rid of the emotional baggage I lugged around at the moment wasn't going to be easy.

"Go on into the fort," Worthington said. "There's an information desk just to the right. The park ranger opened it up for our use. I think one of the other detectives is brewing some coffee."

"I don't drink coffee," I said.

"Sorry, I wasn't thinking. I knew that."

This was the first time I had ever caught Worthington in a lapse. He was rotund and not very inspiring looking for a homicide detective, but appearances meant little. He simply did not forget. Anything that went into his brain stuck there until it was needed again. I'm not a gambling man, but I'd wager odds that Willie Worthington could summon up the details of any case he'd worked on in the past eighteen years on the San Francisco police force.

I took the anklet and the plastic evidence bag into the fort. The arched brick corridor had small windows on either side. I peered through the one on the right and saw the office Worthington had mentioned. Three police officers crowded around the Mr. Coffee.

They turned when I came in. One of them recognized me. "Evening, Mr. Thorne. Did the sarge call you in on this one?"

I silently held up the evidence bag. The man's expression turned neutral.

"You want some peace and quiet?"

"Please." I was already forcing away the pervasive worries that kept me off balance mentally. Another of the officers started to complain about being evicted. It was warm inside, there was a small john in the rear of the office and the supply of decent coffee looked endless. The only other thing he could have needed to think he was in paradise was a doughnut.

The one who had recognized me herded the other two out. I heard their hushed conversation just outside the door, then a loud guffaw. Someone hadn't believed it when he was told why I was here. Psychic crime solvers are mostly frauds.

I wish I was. It would save me a world of emotional hurt.

I prepared myself mentally to enter a world of suicide. Sitting at the desk, I folded my hands over the anklet. There wasn't any need to take it from the plastic evidence bag. The emanations from the metal would pass through the three mil plastic—if there were any vibrations for me to detect.

The wind began to howl outside. I listened and tried to ride along, letting it carry me away from myself. Floating, drifting, I entered a state of light relaxation. Bit by bit I garnered my powers of concentration and, Zenlike, worked hard and did nothing at the same time. The disconnection of spirit and body came slowly, but I did not try to hurry it. The perception of soaring came, and I rocketed skyward without leaving the office.

Aware of both my surroundings and that of the new plane, that misty expanse stretching to infinity in all directions, I began to wander. Time and space are different in this psychometric state. I both hurried and dawdled. Almost as if by accident I found the anklet.

It was still in my hand; now it was in the range of my psychic vision, also.

No!

The pain doubled me over. I slammed my face into the desk but felt nothing. The pain came from lower. My body was being torn apart.

Stop! Don't. Why are you—oh, God, it hurts!

Misery flooded my senses, threatening to drive me insane. Never had I experienced such stark anguish. Pain without limit. Endless, yawning gulfs of agony.

The blade. It's cutting me!

I fell from the chair and writhed on the ground, clutching my middle. The fear clawed at my heart and threatened to rip it from my chest. My throat constricted and my mouth turned to cotton. Terror. Gut-wrenching terror. My worst nightmare stalking me, laughing, torturing me before it began slicing me in half.

Pain! Utter pain!

I began to shake. Tears ran down my cheeks. I tried to force myself away from the anklet. The shaking continued until I thought San Francisco was in the throes of another earthquake. Only then did my eyes pop open. I stared into Willie Worthington's pudgy face.

"Peter, snap out of it. What's happening? Tell me what you're getting off that bracelet."

"Anklet," I corrected weakly. Pushing away, I fought to sit up. It was all illusory, but I had to check my midsection to make sure it was unscathed. There wasn't even a mark on my belly.

"What did you get?" Worthington repeated.

"It . . . it's not a suicide," I managed to choke out. "Not that."

"What is it, then?"

"Torture. She was tortured before someone cut her in half with a huge spinning blade. She was tortured and killed, Willie. God, it was awful."

I vomited again. This time all I had inside me was the last of the antacid tablets. The spasms left me sore and weak—and mentally and emotionally unhinged. I hate it when Worthington forces me into this condition. I would relive the woman's last agonies over and over for days. The only bright spot was having something to displace the uneasiness I'd experienced over the penknife.

And that's not much of a consolation. I stared puking once more, Worthington holding me until I stopped.

CHAPTER 3

My apartment had all the charm of a morgue. I walked in and looked around, trying to figure out why I felt this way tonight. The décor was hardly professional but it suited me. The comfortable upholstered furniture— no leather to stick to—dotting the living room was old and homey. The walls had dozens of large and small vintage lobby posters from the greats of stage magic. The Oriental rug on the floor softened every footstep and made the bottoms of my feet feel cradled and cozy. I turned on the CD player and let the soft, tranquil music of Kindler and Bell's *Dolphin Smiles* surround me.

I settled down on the sofa and stared out the window. My apartment is on the corner of the twentieth floor and has views both north and east, the latter if I care to lean far out on the balcony and look at Coit Tower. The restless waves on the Bay drew me as the music swelled to fill me with—what?

The hollow feeling wouldn't go away. I was alone and that was why my apartment seemed like an alien landscape. I glanced at the VCR's LED display clock and saw that it was almost 1:00 A.M., late to be calling anyone. The telephone is a horrible invention, allowing intrusion into your private life at all times of the day and night. A letter is a communication; a telephone call is an interruption.

I ignored my own thoughts on the matter and punched Barbara Chan's number with quick, sure stabs. Her phone rang three times before she picked it up. I hoped there wouldn't be the uncomfortable jockeying around, the "are you alone?" type of question not being asked but needing an answer. Barbara wasn't my girlfriend. Not exactly. What our relationship was defied easy categorization.

We had met as part of her master's thesis research. She had been investigating psychic phenomena and wanted to quantify my psychometric powers. For whatever reason, mere physical equipment refused to record the vibrations I sensed, and she had gotten nowhere with the project. She had since moved on to another topic and received her degree.

We had seen each other on and off for months, enjoying each other's company and occasionally sleeping together, but there wasn't the kind of spark that made for long-term relationships. Whether it was my fault or hers or simply that the chemistry wasn't right was something I had thought about. There wasn't a good answer other than we made better friends than lovers.

I valued my privacy. I took some small pride in being a loner in a world where everyone shifted relationships constantly, but now that had become a problem. I needed someone. Everything that had happened this evening wore me down like water dripping on a rock for ages. Julianne leaving so unexpectedly was part of it; the penknife she had given me had been the start of my real headache.

Removing the small plastic-handled knife, I tossed it onto the end table. Its hidden psychic message of death and death-giving had unnerved me, but the body—the half body—Worthington had dredged out of the Bay was even more unsettling. The touch of the anklet still burned my hand.

I stared at it and was startled to see the phone.

"Hello?" came Barbara's voice.

"I'm not getting you out of bed, am I?"

"Hi, Peter. Nothing of the sort. I was doing some last-minute packing."

"Packing?" Everyone was going somewhere but me. I was stuck in the middle of a psychic swamp that sucked me deeper with every passing minute. The trapped feeling grew.

"Got an interview back east. It looks as if I might be able to get into Columbia to work on my Ph.D. Dr. Uwani is looking for a graduate assistant and says my recommendations are good. I'm interviewing with him tomorrow—make that this afternoon. I've got to catch the red-eye for New York City in a couple hours."

"Oh."

"Peter, are you all right? You sound weird."

"It's been a rough night," I said. "I lost my assistant and was hoping to persuade you to fill in for a couple shows until I could get a replacement."

"Sorry, wish I could." Barbara paused. "That would be a real kick, wouldn't it? I've never been onstage professionally."

"People would be watching you."

"I'd have to wear that skimpy outfit, wouldn't I?"

"You look good in it."

"And you've told me I looked good out of my clothes." Her tone was light and bantering. This was the kind of response I needed.

"You do. You'd be doing me a big favor since you know some of the tricks. I wouldn't have to take a raw recruit and try to turn her into an expert in a few hours."

Barbara hesitated, then said, "I'd really like to, Peter. If you had called a couple days ago, I'd've jumped at the chance. You know how I am. Always trying new things. But I can't. This interview is important."

"It means you're moving to New York." I was happy for her even as I felt increasingly sorry for myself.

"I hope so. It won't be forever. I can't see living in a place like New York. Ugly place. I'll be coming back as soon as I get my Ph.D. I *like* San Francisco."

"And you could probably get a teaching position here if you received your Ph.D. at some other school."

"Universities don't like putting their own graduates on their faculty," she said. "It makes sense. It keeps small dynasties from growing. Columbia is a topnotch school." She paused again. "There's something else bothering you, isn't there, Peter?"

"It's not important. I'd hoped you could come over tonight, or that I could drive over to your place." Barbara lived in Oakland not far from UC even though she had gotten her master's degree from the University of San Francisco.

"Has Worthington dumped another murder on you? That fat son of a bitch. I know how hard it is for you to shake that off. Are you all right?"

"I'm fine," I lied. "I was just wanting to see you. I'd better not keep you if your flight leaves soon. Will you be leaving from San Francisco International?"

"No, I've got a flight out of Oakland. It was cheaper."

"Have a good flight," I said. "And here's hoping you get the assistantship."

"It's a cinch, Peter." Barbara paused again before saying, "Are you *sure* you're okay?"

"You worry about me too much. Worry about Uwani."

"He's an old curmudgeon," Barbara said, "but he's nothing like Dr. Michaelson. I can get along with Uwani. I better go, Peter. You take care of yourself and don't let Worthington saddle you with anything you can't handle."

"I won't. See you when you get back."

"It's a date."

She hung up. I listened for a moment until the shrill beep-beep-beeping started. I replaced the phone. A call is an interruption, not a communication. The short talk with Barbara had confirmed this. I got up and went to the window and watched the ships working their way across the Bay.

Closing my eyes for a moment, I heard the dead woman's shrill screams as she died. I shivered and tried to keep the psychic chill from freezing me. Being with a dying person is different from sharing their innermost thoughts and emotions as they die. It's always difficult to watch someone you know die; it's worse being inside a stranger's head and heart and experiencing everything she does as she expires.

I turned from the window and knew it wouldn't be possible for me to get any sleep tonight. I opened the sliding door, went out on the balcony, and leaned out as far as I could to look east. Staring past San Francisco toward the lights of Berkeley crawling halfway up the side of the mountains I wondered if I would ever see Barbara Chan again. She might rush back, pack her few belongings, and be off for New York City, and never even have lunch with me. I couldn't blame her. We were friends.

I needed more than a friend at the moment.

The wind whipping across the city chilled my body even as the memory of the psychometry froze my soul. A sadist with a knife and woman who had died by being cut in half. I shuddered, not knowing if it was body or mind causing the reaction.

I resolutely forced myself to relax, almost a contradiction. Rather than denying the thoughts and feelings I had, I accepted them and let them flow across my spirit like a gelid river. Relaxation didn't come but a measure of peace did. In the morning I'd have to find a new assistant since I had subconsciously come to the decision not to cancel the act. I had never done that before and wouldn't now, even if I had to wing it alone. An assistant was useful but not necessary. Many beginning stage magicians perform all the time without an assistant.

I went back inside and sprawled on my bed, letting sleep overtake me. I was relaxed and at peace.

The nightmares started an hour later and stalked me every time my eyelids closed. It was a long and tiring night filled with the woman's hideous screams as she died over and over in my head.

CHAPTER 4

Saturday morning isn't the best time to start looking for a stage assistant, but I had no choice. I hadn't gotten much sleep so I rested until eight o'clock and began calling. It went pretty much as I had feared. Experience counted in today's world and came at a premium. I would have gladly paid it for a trained and knowledgeable assistant. By ten o'clock I would have paid anything.

The only people in town were solidly under contract. I couldn't even "borrow" anyone for a single evening. I sat back and stared out the window toward the Bay. My thoughts drifted back to the emotional gash that Worthington's floater had ripped across my mind. I forced myself to return to business. It was more immediate, I had a reputation at stake, and there was damned little I could do but brood over the dead woman's last few minutes.

There was no indication of who had tortured her to death, nor was there even a small hint of where the murder had occurred. All I had done for Worthington was to complicate his life by telling him the woman hadn't jumped from the Golden Gate Bridge and hadn't run afoul of a ship's huge propeller after dying in the water. How Worthington was supposed to find the other half of her body wasn't my problem.

Living with the knowledge that she had died so hideously was my problem. Every breath I took carried some small portion of the agony she had suffered during her last passionate moments of life.

I walked out on the balcony and stared toward Oakland. That was another of my problems without a real solution. By now Barbara Chan was in New York, maybe having her interview with the Columbia professor. I wished her well, but I also wished I could either want her a bit more distant from my life or be more comfortable with her playing a greater role in it. Neither route seemed likely. She had a life of her own, and now I had to believe I might never see her again. We might even be reduced to sending each other insincere cards at Christmas saying ''We've got to get together soon.''

''Think,'' I muttered out loud. ''Who can help? Who knows everyone in town? In the university drama departments, or where out-of-work actresses get together. How I can contact the one who'll work as my assistant?''

All I needed was someone to fill in for one night. Tomorrow was Sunday and I could always round up someone given the extra twenty-four hours. A single ad in the following Sunday classifieds might be all I'd need to be inundated by applicants on Monday morning, a week too late.

''Almost eleven,'' I grumbled. ''Who knows everyone worth knowing in San Francisco?'' I turned from the view of the Bay Bridge and went back inside, mind working feverishly. By the time I sat down next to the phone, I had my answer. Gloria Gadsen ran a downtown art gallery. The people she didn't know didn't matter. I looked up the Gadsen Gallery number and quickly punched it in. I waited impatiently as the beeps came back to me, putting the call through.

''Gadsen Gallery, how may I help you?'' came the immediate, if cool, response.

''This is Peter Thorne,'' I said. ''I'd like to speak with Gloria, if she's free.''

''One moment, Mr. Thorne.''

I fumed as I listened to the damned elevator music over the phone when I was put on hold. Time stretched endlessly while Dylan's ''The Times They Are A-

Changin' " was masticated into monotonous pablum. Gloria Gadsen finally came on the line.

"Peter, this is a coincidence. I was just talking about you. Are your ears burning?"

"Just my bloodshot eyes," I said. "It's been a long night."

"I imagine they all are for an attractive man like you. You ought to save some time for me."

"Always the flirt, aren't you, Gloria?"

"When you reach my age, that's all you have left. And don't prattle on about me not being that old. Why, I'm old enough to be your . . . older sister."

I had to smile. Gloria Gadsen was in her early sixties and elegant in the way only age brings.

"Well, Sis," I said, "since we're family, you might be able to do me a favor."

"A favor, Peter?" A sly note had crept into her voice. "I'm sure I might be able to arrange something—but only if you were able to reciprocate."

"Even better, Gloria. I'm willing to pay for this." I explained my need for a temporary assistant until I could find one able to take the job on a long-term basis.

"I have just the person for you, Peter. She's tall, almost as tall as you—you're six feet, aren't you?"

"A fraction over," I said.

"Michelle is five-ten and has the look of a model. Long, dark hair, wonderful blue eyes. You do like blue eyes, don't you, Peter?"

"I need an assistant, not someone to meet all my personal preferences in a woman."

"But you do like midnight black hair and blue eyes?"

I admitted that I did.

"Good, then it's settled. Michelle is the one for you."

"I'd have to see how she moves, how she works with tricks. I'd prefer someone who was athletic. They tend to have a sureness about their movements that lets them learn more easily."

"You're very athletic, aren't you, Peter? I mean, you

didn't get those broad shoulders and tight rear end sitting around on Sundays swilling beer and watching the football game on TV.''

"I work out regularly," I said. It was a necessity for my act. Strength and control were inseparable. And when I got back to doing escapes and other stunts, being in top physical condition was the only way to keep from getting into serious trouble. Even then it was no guarantee. I shuddered as I remembered back eight years when I tried the Houdini water can escape.

I had three assistants then and have been grateful ever since that they knew their jobs. I had been unable to get out of the straitjacket while still in the water-filled can. A sudden cramp had caused me to suck in some water. I would have died then and there if they hadn't used axes to destroy the can. As it was, I sustained the brain damage that caused my psychometric powers to appear.

Swallowing hard, I tried to force away the rising tide of torment still lingering after last night's psychometry. Worthington thought I was a freak but he hid his opinion well, at least in my presence. A freak I might be, but cursed seems a more appropriate description of the power. I had to *live* over and over every instant of the most horrendous experience of a woman's life.

"Michelle will be perfect. She might even want to train for a longer stretch. She tried to get onto Broadway, but there wasn't much call for dancers—not the kind of dancing she wanted to do."

"What's that?"

"With at least a few stitches of clothing on," Gloria said primly. I tried to picture Gloria Gadsen being the proper parent and failed.

"Who is this Michelle?" I asked.

"Michelle Ferris. She's my youngest niece, and I promised her mother I'd look after her out here in Baghdad by the Bay. What do you say, Peter? Is she what you're looking for?"

"She sounds too good to be true," I answered. And

she did. A dancer meant she was used to being onstage and wasn't likely to freeze when the spotlight hit her. Her height and physical attributes were also plus factors—unless Gloria was embellishing. Even if she was, I was willing to give her niece a trial for one night. I was desperate.

"Michelle is one in a million."

I didn't point out that that meant there were two hundred fifty others like her in the United States. Numbers changed faster than old clichés.

"When do I meet her? I've got to work with her this afternoon to be ready for an eight o'clock performance at the Rialto."

"You're working for that detestable Barry Morgan? I'm surprised at you, Peter. I thought you had more class."

"He pays top dollar."

"Hmm," Gloria said. "I'd need your promise that you'd keep Michelle away from that filthy old reprobate."

"No problem," I said, still overjoyed that I had a possible for my assistant. Michelle would have to have both smallpox and the Black Plague before I'd turn her down.

"Very well. Michelle will be here at the gallery around noon. Come by then, Peter. And we can discuss payment then."

"I said I'd go top scale and I meant it."

"For Michelle, you'll pay it. I'll see to that, but I meant *my* payment. Remember, it's always the middleman who gets rich. That's how H. L. Hunt made his billions."

"If you're her agent, you probably shouldn't take more than twenty percent," I said.

"She gets to keep every penny you pay her," Gloria Gadsen said. "This is just between you and me. I don't think you'll find the pay too onerous." She cackled like the Wicked Witch of the West.

"Noon," I said. "See you then." I hung up, wondering what payment Gloria was likely to extract. At the moment, no price was too high.

The Gadsen Galley was on Maiden Lane just a few yards off Union Square. I parked in the underground lot and walked quickly through the noontime pedestrians. On a Saturday the traffic was at a minimum for a regular calendar day. The only times I ever see fewer people around is on a holiday. Then the Saks and I. Magnin and other big stores are closed and there's no reason for anyone but a dyed-in-the-wool tourist to come to this area.

I swung around the wrought-iron railing and took the steps down to Gloria's gallery two at a time. I didn't want to hurry but couldn't help myself. The need to see Michelle Ferris and scope out her possibilities as an assistant were overwhelming.

There was also an added reason for the rush and the preoccupation with the unseen niece. It kept my mind busy. If I relaxed for too long, the psychic impressions rose in my mind and sent red-hot bolts of terror through me.

"Yes?" The receptionist in the gallery gave me a once-over and instantly decided I wasn't the type who bought art from Gloria Gadsen. I had to admire such swift appraisal since it was true. My tastes run to Hiroshige prints and Erté sculpture rather than nonobjectivist art.

"Ms. Gadsen is expecting me," I said.

"Mr. Thorne?" She spoke as if the words burned her lips. "Yes, she is expecting you. She and her niece are in the upstairs office. This way, please."

She moved lithely from behind the reception desk and gave me a nice view as she made her way up a spiral wrought-iron staircase. I was beginning to think that if Michelle Ferris didn't work out, Gloria's receptionist might.

"Peter!" came Gloria Gadsen's greeting. "You're so prompt. That's a good trait. You don't often see it in people these days. I schedule private showings and clients are *hours* late. It is so exasperating.''

I hoped the woman seated in the comfortable chair to Gloria's right was her niece. She had a slightly frightened air to her that was more than offset by her good looks. She would be perfect as an assistant, even if she did no more than move a few of the tricks on- and offstage.

"I see you've already given Michelle the once-over. Isn't she all I promised, Peter?''

"Ms. Ferris, pleased to make your acquaintance. I hope your aunt hasn't pushed you into something you'd rather not do.''

"I do need a job, Mr. Thorne.''

"Such formality!'' exclaimed Gloria Gadsen. "Do call each other by your first names. Loosen up, Peter, Michelle. There's no need to be so uptight.''

"Aunt Gloria, please. Don't meddle.''

"That's her way,'' I said, ignoring Gloria. "But in this case, I think I'm happy she did. Has she explained my predicament?''

Michelle nodded.

"There's more to the job than just looking pretty, though I have to admit you do a great job of that.''

"Chauvinist pig,'' mumbled Gloria. I glanced in her direction and she smiled sweetly.

"She's right. It's part of the showmanship needed for stage magic. Distractions are vital. Here, let me show you.'' I pulled a deck of cards from my pocket and riffled through them.

"Should I take one?''

"Go on. This is a simple trick. It doesn't matter what one you choose,'' I said. "I'll always be able to pick it after you've looked at it and put it back into the deck.''

She pulled out one, examined it carefully, and then put it back into the pack. I made a big deal out of looking away. It wasn't necessary but it added a certain something to the trick. I ran my finger along the edge of the deck and with a quick motion, fanned the cards and chose the four of diamonds. Michelle took the card and examined the intricate pattern on the back as if it might be marked. Then she said, ''Are they all the same card?''

I fanned them face up to show her that they weren't.

''Shuffle them again.'' Michelle watched closely. I worked slowly, not trying to hide what I did but not being obvious either. Again she chose a card when I fanned the deck for her. She just glanced at it, already understanding this was of no importance to the trick. I made sure she inserted the card in the lower portion of the deck.

''There's a thread through the deck,'' she said suddenly. ''Let me try.''

It took several tries but she finally mastered the technique of slipping the card reinserted into the deck against the thread. Careful tension on the black thread made the chosen card slip slightly out of the deck. All it took was a quick flick and the card could always be produced. The only real skill this trick took was not shuffling the bottom quarter of the deck where the cards were fastened together by the thread.

I watched with some appreciation as Michelle's fingers stroked the deck and manipulated them. She was far from expert, but she had strong hands and moved well. The quickness and dexterity were there, if untrained. This boded well for several of the stunts in my current act. She'd have to concentrate to make them work right, but she was quick on the uptake. I didn't think it would give her any problem and I told her.

''So?'' asked Gloria Gadsen. ''Is she hired?''

''We'll have to spend the afternoon in some intensive training, but my hopes for Michelle are higher than they've been for any of my other assistants—and some have been in the business for years.''

Michelle blushed at the compliment. I couldn't remember the last time I'd seen a woman do that. I would have to ask more about her short career as a dancer.

Hoofers as a group swear like longshoremen and are not embarrassed by anything.

"Before you two run off to practice the act," Gloria said, "I'm going to call in my marker."

"So soon?"

"Of course, Peter. I never let moss grow under the north side of my rolling stone, or however that old saying went. I need you to put on a short performance tomorrow evening."

"Tomorrow?" I was disappointed. Sunday was my only day off. Still, it was small enough price to pay. "What's the occasion?"

"I've got a hot new artist I'm featuring in the gallery. His work is simply the best since Picasso, and I've invited everyone to the opening."

"And? I'm not a critic."

"No, but you're an entertainer. I want you to circulate, do a few magic tricks, keep them amused."

"Don't think your new artist's work will totally enthrall them?"

"Peter, really. You know it's not like that. Fashion designers put on lavish entertainment extravaganzas for their new lines. There's no reason an art opening can't share some of that festivity. Give them something to dazzle their senses, first with your magic and then with Taggart's oils."

"Taggart's your discovery?" I frowned. I thought I had heard of him but couldn't remember where.

"He's good, Peter, damned good. But frankly, you're much better with people than he is. He takes the artist-as-iconoclast far too seriously."

"I remember him now," I said. "He was arrested a few months ago when he punched out an art critic."

"Paul said some absolutely terrible things about Taggart and his work. It was personal. Paul is, well, he likes the company of other males. Taggart wouldn't have anything to do with him. That sparked the animosity. And in all fairness, I don't think Paul liked Taggart's work. His tastes tend more to the French Impressionists.''

"I'll do it on one condition," I said.

Gloria Gadsen got a vexed look. "Well. What is it?"

"Michelle works with me. I'll need an assistant to do your opening properly."

I saw by Michelle Ferris's broad smile that this was fine with her, too. Things were definitely looking up.

CHAPTER 5

"I don't mind getting started," Michelle said. "If the show is tonight at eight, there's not that much time to put in a little bit of practice."

"Let's go then. If you don't mind, Gloria?" I found myself distracted by my planning and not ready to deal with her anymore. She was a take-charge sort who could wrangle a deal from the devil better than anyone I knew. I wanted to leave before she got my soul, too.

"Not at all. Just don't get so wrapped up in everything that you forget tomorrow night, Peter. I'm counting on you."

"I'm sure you are," I said. I waited for Michelle to leave first. As we went down the spiral staircase a thought hit me.

"We've got to make a small side trip, but I think it might be useful in your magical education," I said to her. I had forgotten that I was supposed to witness a séance this afternoon. There was plenty of time to make it. And I thought it might give Michelle a closer look at how tricks were done in the real world.

"I don't understand," Michelle said when I told her we had to spend an hour or so at the séance. "Aunt Gloria said you don't believe in spiritualism."

"I don't. That's part of the reason I started doing a bit of debunking. You might say I'm following in Houdini's footsteps."

"I still don't—"

The street people flocked like gnats around us. Before I got to the parking garage, I'd run through all my quarters and was thinking about asking Michelle for some change. Ever since some judge decided that they have a constitutional right not only to ask for spare change but to be physically aggressive about it, downtown San Francisco hasn't been the same. I can't imagine how tourists from the great heartland react to having street people, badly in need of washing and dental care, press up against them and radiate a forty-horsepower breath when they are extorting change. A good beggar can make as much as two hundred tax-free dollars a day.

Urban problems abounded, but the city was still a good place to live.

"Houdini wanted to believe in the survival of the soul but never found a medium who was legitimate. I know there are powers other than the usual ones granted humans. I'd like to find them and get some handle on why I can psychometrize."

"But you said you were debunking these people."

I didn't want to get into the history: being a guinea pig for Barbara Chan's experiment and the way her adviser had been so antagonistic. Even in the face of my talent, he had never believed. His mind was as set as those who believe without any real proof. Mental powers other than the ones he had couldn't exist. Period. That was the limit to his universe and anything flying against it had to be a fraud.

I took a different approach. I wanted to find a legitimate medium able to channel or draw power from a crystal or even display the same powers I had. I wanted it—and I also wanted to be sure that the con artists weren't preying on the gullible. In a way, it was penance for my own psychometry talent.

"What do you look for?"

"I approach it as a stage magician looking for gimmicks. If you do the same, you might be able to figure out how the spirit voices speak and so on."

"How many times have you done this?"

"As I said, I just started. This will be number eight or nine." I shuddered as I remembered one medium

who had called herself Lady MacDowell—Lady
MacBeth would have been closer.

"Is anything wrong, Mr. Thorne?"

"Peter," I corrected absently. I wheeled the Bimmer
up the ramp and onto Grant and drove down to Market.
My mind got caught up in one of those damned feed-
back loops that drove me crazy. I couldn't get Lady
MacDowell out of my mind now that Michelle had triggered the memory.

"The séance was a fraud, wasn't it? The one that's
bothering you so?"

I turned and looked at her. She was quick to see what
was agitating me so much. Her blue eyes were almost
enough to pull me into her soul and let me lose myself.

"Lady MacDowell," I said, "was a crook. There
wasn't a question about that from the first few minutes.
She had the place rigged—and it wasn't even very
clever. I exposed her and gave her my usual ultimatum.
Get out of town in twenty-four hours or I file a report
with the police."

"What happened?"

"Everything blew up in her face. Two of the others
at the same séance had lost considerable sums of money
to her. More than a thousand each from their reactions.
They didn't go to the cops but they weren't too pleasant."

"Then she was ruined in San Francisco. It would
only make sense to move on," Michelle said.

"She had tangled with people who had connections
all over the place. She'd have to start from scratch with
a new identity and scam." I shrugged. Most bunco
artists wouldn't mind that. Their names were changed
more often than their underwear. Lady MacDowell
hadn't been too stable mentally, though.

"And?"

Michelle was determined to get the story from me. I
sighed and finished it. "She committed suicide. It was
a messy way to go, too. Not the usual way. She got ten
sticks of dynamite and detonated it."

"How do you know it wasn't one of the clients she had bilked who had her killed?"

"She left a suicide note. A quite explicit one, too, naming me as the reason she offed herself." I shuddered. "Willie Worthington called me to the scene since he was the investigating officer. He showed me the note—there was no question she had written it. And I did a bit of psychometry. She was responsible for making the mess." I didn't even have to close my eyes to picture the blood and flesh spattered against the brick walls in the old warehouse where Lady MacDowell had killed herself. It had been spectacularly bloody.

"There wasn't any question she was dead?"

"None. My psychometry showed she was the one who died. Worthington took it on faith that I was right. It cleared a case quickly for him."

"You're not blaming yourself for her death, are you, Peter?"

"No, not really," I said, not knowing if this was the strict truth. The sight of so much blood and gore dried on the brick walls of that dusty warehouse was the stuff of horror movies.

I drove to the Mission District and found a parking place on a side street without too much trouble. A woman concerned over her medium's claims of spirit healing had contacted me. She was a diabetic looking for a cure to a condition science could only treat. I didn't think she was going to get any permanent relief from Magyar the Hungarian, but I tried to keep my mind open.

"There's our contact," I said, seeing Mary Kerkorian in a doorway. The elderly woman looked upset. I hoped that nothing had happened to her. Dealing with bunco artists is relatively safe, but the occasional one turns violent when their scams are exposed.

Some, like Lady MacDowell, even become self-destructive.

"Peter, I'm so glad you made it. I was worried you wouldn't come."

"What's wrong, Mrs. Kerkorian? You're very upset."

"You know that little girl who has been coming to the sessions? The one I told you about?"

"The woman with leukemia? I remember." I was aware of Michelle pressing closer to hear.

"She's stopped her chemotherapy to be able to pay Magyar his fee. She says the doctors can't do anything but slow the cancer and that Magyar can cure it."

"That's risky. Do you believe Magyar's claims about being a healer?"

"I . . ." She squared her shoulders and finally shook her head. "I've thought about it. No, I don't believe him anymore. I want to—I wanted to, but I can't. The look on his face is so, is so avaricious when he talks to that poor girl."

"What does he have on tap for today?"

"He's doing another psychic healing. Some sort of tumor."

"Do you know the patient?"

The gray-haired woman shook her head. I turned to Michelle and said, "This one's likely to be pretty bloody. It might be better if I went in by myself."

"No!" Michelle was adamant. "I want to see. This is so different from anything I've done. Aunt Gloria always tells me I ought to get out and *do* things rather than being an idle spectator. This is a good chance to see how con artists work."

"I'm afraid that's right," I said. "Let's get it over."

Mrs. Kerkorian led the way, Michelle and me trailing a little behind her. The houses in the area were mostly two-story frame. An occasional adobe with a landmark medallion on its wall gave a hint of the Spanish heritage of the area. We went up the back stairs of an ill-kept house. Mrs. Kerkorian knocked. The door opened without apparent human assistance.

A slight breeze from inside carried the heavy smell of incense. My nose twitched and began to drip a little, but I went in. I paused to let my eyes adjust to the darkness. Mediums claim they need the dim lighting to concentrate. The ones I've had occasion to encounter need it to hide the mechanisms that provide them their spiritual illusions. If they were even half-good stage magicians they could perform in bright light and no one would ever catch on to their tricks.

"Where do we go?" asked Michelle, her voice low. She seemed apprehensive. I put my hand on her arm to reassure her. Instead of calming her, it made her jump.

"Sorry," I said. "Just follow Mrs. Kerkorian." We made our way through folds of cloth cunningly set to form a long passage where none really existed. By the time we reached the audience chamber, it felt as if we might have hiked halfway to San Jose. Already seated at the table were a half dozen others, three men and three women. Mrs. Kerkorian went to sit beside one pale woman, obviously the source of her concern over Magyar's abilities.

"We have those among us who are ill," came a resonant voice. I looked around and located the most likely spot for the hidden speakers. Magyar used a decent stereo system. There wasn't any bass rumble. When the high-pitch squealing started, there wouldn't be any hysteresis overload, either.

"Let's sit down," I said, guiding both Michelle and Mrs. Kerkorian to chairs at the end of the table. The farther from where Magyar sat the better I liked it. Too close and the stunts were hidden. This gave both distance and a chance to see anyone moving behind the medium.

I wondered how many assistants Magyar employed and why it was so easy for crooks to find them. If it hadn't been for Michelle, I might have asked the medium to borrow one or two of his helpers for my evening performance.

A sudden gust of wind whipped through the chamber. With it came a stomach-turning scent intended to distract my attention. I squinted against the tears forming and saw two careless hands poking through the dark hanging curtains behind the unoccupied chair at the other end of the oval table.

As if by magic, the curtains parted and Magyar strutted out. He was a small man, swarthy and heavily bearded. His mustache drooped and his black hair was caught up with tiny jeweled pins that caught the faint light and made it appear as if a halo formed around his head. A disturbing subsonic sound rose up until it was almost audible, then died. The deep rumbling made my inner organs feel as if they were bouncing against one another.

It was an impressive entrance. I wondered if I could get by with using the subsonic assault in my own act to build tension. I doubted it. The government frowned on introducing gases into the audience to increase laughter, and there had always been a hue and cry about subliminals, even though nothing had ever been done to outlaw them.

"There are those among us who are seriously ill. Magyar will heal one of them—now!"

One emaciated man across the table rose as if in a trance and walked around until he stood at the medium's elbow. Magyar stared straight ahead. The subsonic rumbling began again and grated at my ears until I was ready to scream. Michelle did when the sudden cessation caught her by surprise.

Magyar took the small shriek in stride. It meant his assistants were doing their job.

"The table in front of me," he intoned, holding out both his arms. "Lie there. Allow me to examine you psychically."

The man looked more like a zombie than a living being. He was gaunt to the point of starvation. He climbed onto the table and lay staring at the draped ceilings. Only now and then did he blink. If the others hadn't been watching him as closely as I was, they might never have seen the slow flutter of his eyelids.

"The spiritual need is upon me," cried Magyar.

''Give me the power. I need the power to heal! Give it to me, give it to *me*!''

He flapped his sleeves. I was looking at the ceiling. I saw the red pendant being lowered on the thin black thread. I jumped when the laser caught the red crystal and sent lambent rays spinning around the room. It was the same effect of spinning a silver, multi-faceted ball in a dance hall. Nevertheless, it was very effective. The red and green and yellow beams swung around the room as the red crystal slowly twisted on the thread.

''The power of my mind reaches out to study the festering inner sickness I sense.'' Magyar placed his hands on the man's chest. With a quick motion, the medium ripped open the man's shirt, sending buttons skittering along the table. Michelle followed the buttons; I watched the curtains behind Magyar.

I thought I caught sight of a laser as new beams were focused on the crystal. The rays bounced down and bathed the medium's hands in blue-green light. Magyar began rubbing vigorously, moaning and crying out that he was discovering the cause of the man's sickness.

''Cancer. He has a tumor that can be removed psychically.'' Magyar moved around the table. I tried to see if there was anything behind him but couldn't. He had positioned himself so that the man on the table blocked my direct line of sight. Unless I wanted to stand and make myself obvious, I'd have to be content with just watching. It hardly mattered. What happened now was old hat.

That didn't make it any less disgusting—or astounding looking.

Both Michelle and Mrs. Kerkorian gasped when Magyar began rubbing the man's chest and started pulling out a bloody tumor.

''The spirits aid me. The power channeled from my Gypsy ancestors flows through me. I know the old ways. I know the healing arts, the ways of healing that have been forgotten or denied. I am cleansing his body of the cancer!''

Magyar jerked away, the repulsive piece of chicken gizzard in his hand. He held it aloft as it were a war trophy.

"I have psychically removed the tumor. You are no longer ill. Rise and be well in body and spirit."

The man sat up, looking dazed. He touched the bloody streak on his chest as if he didn't believe it.

"I feel fine," he said in a low voice. Louder, he cried, "I'm healed. The cancer is gone. The doctors said they couldn't cure me, but the cancer's gone!"

"There are others here who are ill. Mrs. Kerkorian. Your diabetes is rampant. I feel its evil flooding your system. You have purified yourself as I instructed?"

"Yes!" she almost cried. "I've done everything you said."

Michelle gripped my hand under the table.

"Wait," I said in a low voice. "She's caught up in the healing."

"Look into the crystal," Magyar said. "What do you see?"

"I—nothing. There's nothing there."

"Look deeply. Believe. Believe!"

From the depths of the crystal came a light yellow glow. It grew in intensity until I saw a distinct scene in 3-D. Somehow Magyar was able to project a hologram using the crystal as a screen. I saw where the second laser had to be placed.

"I believe. I see it!" Mrs. Kerkorian rose.

So did I. I spun and yanked hard at the drapery behind her. The black cloth tumbled to the floor to reveal the man hunching over the laser. Magyar's surprised assistant straightened, a heavy glass slide in his hand.

"There's your pastoral scene," I said. "It's only a hologram that's being projected through the crystal. It's a neat trick, but there's nothing psychic about it."

I swung through the room, a comet hurling through space and toward the illumination of the sun. Yanking at the heavy curtains revealed another man with the second laser. I pushed back the drapes behind Magyar and exposed a woman dressed in black. I didn't know what she was going to do, but it would have been apparent if we had gone on with the fake psychic healing session.

"What's the meaning of this? You're destroying my channel."

"I'll destroy more than that," I growled. Magyar was short but stocky. I topped him by six inches but he had the weight on me. In a fight, it could get nasty.

"Get the hell out of here," he shouted. "You're disturbing my—"

"I'm exposing your scam," I said. "Let's see your hands." I caught Magyar's wrists and jerked them up. Stage magicians use special pouches strapped to their arms to hide items that eventually appear "magically." In his case, Magyar had a great deal up his sleeve.

"There," cried Mrs. Kerkorian, "There's another tumor."

"Chicken gizzard," I said. "He was going to palm another chicken gizzard and make it seem as if he were pulling it out of another cancer victim." I looked around the table. A woman put her hand to her mouth and looked faint. From the pallor she must be suffering from a cancer, probably inoperable. Magyar would have "psychically cured" her, bilking her of her money and leaving her deadly cancer untreated.

Stealing from the gullible is one thing. Stealing money from the terminally ill is even lower.

"How's your patient, Magyar?" I reached back with my left hand and collared the gaunt man who had been operated on. He tried to pull free, his strength belying his appearance.

"You don't have nothing on me, Thorne. Lemme go."

"As I live and breathe," I said. "Lester Hill. Not enough purses to snatch out at Pier Thirty-nine these days?"

"You don't have nothin' on me."

"Ladies and gentleman, this fine soul is a petty

thief." I turned back to Magyar. "And this one is a big thief."

"You were going to charge me ten thousand dollars," the pale woman gasped.

"Even petty thieves can be ill," Magyar said. "I had no idea who he was."

I snorted, then released his arm. "Here's how he did it." I reached out and grabbed Magyar's head and pulled him close. He struggled. As he fought, I drew my hand slowly along his neck. Blood squirted out and the chicken gizzard I'd taken from his pouch slowly oozed from between my fingers.

"Were you cancerous, Magyar? Why not heal yourself? I'll tell you why. It's a trick. It's all a scam."

"Go to hell!"

"He's a fraud," another woman said. When Mrs. Kerkorian went to comfort her, I knew she was the object of this farce. "He would have stolen my money and let me die!"

"We'll take care of him," I said. I kept a firm grip on Magyar's sleeve. The police are often accused of being elbow fetishists, but hanging on to a suspect's elbow is a good way of controlling him. A slight lift and the weight changes on the toes, making it impossible to run or fight effectively.

"I want the police," the woman said. "I want him in jail!"

"Michelle, stop Lester. He's trying to get away. He's not too dangerous." I watched as Michelle Ferris raced after the gaunt man. I heard a small scuffle and then saw her coming back with him. Lester wasn't a violent sort and wouldn't put up a fight. I had seen him cowed by children eight and nine years old.

"The others are as responsible as I am," Magyar said, still struggling. I wondered how much longer it would be before he tried to punch me. It had to occur to him that Mrs. Kerkorian and her friend with leukemia were going to press bunco charges. The best he could hope for was to cop a plea to a lesser charge and maybe do six months in the county jail.

"I'm sure they are, but we have you, not them."

"I'll phone the police," Michelle offered.

"What's it going to be, ladies?" I wanted them to make up their minds. They were the ones who would have to bear the brunt of the emotional confrontation in court. Magyar's attorney would make them out to be fools and worse. They would be portrayed as patrons of the art of channeling, out for nothing more than a lark.

I read all this on Mrs. Kerkorian's face. Then she looked at her friend and the expression changed from one of inconvenience to determination. She wanted Magyar behind bars for what he had done.

"Call them," I said. At the same time, I changed my grip on Magyar. He tried to wiggle free. I caught his hand and bent it back in a come-along that would break his wrist if he struggled. "And then we've got work to do."

Michelle grinned as she went to find the phone, still hanging onto Lester's collar.

CHAPTER 6

The stage at the Rialto was barren and cold. A half-hearted cleaning had occurred sometime during the late morning after the play, and dust still hung in the air. I found the entire place depressing, but I had to spend some time here if I wanted Michelle to get the idea of what we had to do in less than six hours.

"I can't believe it, Peter," she said as I fiddled with the small table holding Morgan's damned animals. The small lion cub was sometimes vicious and had tried to maul me. I used a heavy wire-mesh glove to soothe him. He was out of sorts, and little wonder. Everyone around him was being one royal pain in the ass. Why shouldn't he enjoy biting the hand that fed him?

Heaven knew that Morgan himself relished this very prospect on a daily basis. He never tired of baiting me, of demanding new and more obscure elements in my act, of inventing problems for me to overcome. I was glad my run at the theater was about over. Morgan paid well, but not so well that I needed to put up with him much longer.

"What?" I asked absentmindedly. I was thinking about the act and figuring where Michelle ought to stand for maximum effect—and maximum hiding of my sleight of hand.

"I've never done anything like this afternoon before. I was responsible for having a con artist arrested. You always hear how citizens ought to do more to stop crime. This afternoon, I *did*!"

"Lester is hardly a top-of-the-line crook," I said, fixing the hidden trap that would release the lion cub and swallow the two pigeons simultaneously. ''As for Magyar, the cops will have him up on all kinds of charges, but they won't amount to a hill of beans. I've seen cases like this before.''

''What do you mean?'' Michelle came over and watched as I oiled the hinges to keep them from making any noise. I opened and closed the trap several times to be sure it functioned perfectly. If the lion cub was trapped under the table for a second night in a row, it would put up one whale of a roar and spoil the illusion.

''He'll plea bargain down to a misdemeanor. Mrs. Kerkorian is all fired up now. So is her friend with leukemia, but their ire will die down in a few weeks or months.''

''So?''

''Magyar won't come to trial for a year or longer. There's a good chance Mrs. Kerkorian's friend will be dead by then. If she's dead, she can't appear as a witness against Magyar.''

''She can give a deposition.''

I shrugged it off. The courts were too busy to listen to swindled women's statements, especially if they were dead. This was why I preferred running con artists out of town. They'd set up their scam somewhere else, but it got them out of San Francisco. Since it often took considerable time and money to put on a good scam, this treatment was also a kind of punishment.

''You don't have to do this, Peter. Why do you take the time if there's no real punishment for the likes of Magyar?''

I didn't want to explain my real reason to Michelle. My wife had died five years ago from cancer. She went to a crooked astrologer who told her to trust only a psychic healer. Medical treatment might not have saved her life, but it could have made her last days less painful. I held her death against both the faith healer and the astrologer, whether irrational or justified I was in no position to say. But I wanted to see every fake psychic healer run out of town on a rail, since modern society frowned on tarring and feathering.

"Here's your spot. I've got it marked with a cross of white tape. Always go from white to yellow to red and then back." Mentally I ran through the order of the tricks. Michelle would always be moving to a position to block me from the audience when I needed the shielding the most. Half the tricks I did required a few seconds setup time while onstage. My assistant was needed to give me that time.

"Do you want me to—" Michelle stopped when she saw someone moving around out in the empty theater.

I turned. I was afraid it might be the manager coming to scope out my new assistant. Even if I hadn't promised Gloria that her niece would be safe from Morgan, I'd have done my damnedest to keep them apart. Morgan was a lecher whom I would cheerfully drop off a tall building.

"Sorry to interrupt your rehearsal, Peter," came a voice I knew all too well. "This your new assistant? You do have an eye for the ladies. She's a stunner."

Willie Worthington waddled up onto the stage, the short flight of steps creaking under his weight. He puffed and panted from the slight exertion as he came over. He shook hands with Michelle, his pudgy fingers lingering in hers for a moment.

"Soft hands, too. You in the business?" he asked.

"I tried out as a dancer back in New York," Michelle said. "I didn't get very far. I came out here and—"

"Detective Worthington, do you need to interrogate her as if she were suspect?"

"Don't get so testy, Peter. I was just making polite conversation."

I turned to Michelle and said, "Detective Sergeant Worthington does *not* make small talk. Everything you say is filed away and remembered, seemingly forever. He will use it against you when you least expect it."

"You both malign and flatter me, Peter. You've got a pretty decent memory yourself. Has he shown you that mentalist trick of his where he reads a list of non-sense words and numbers, then recites them back? Dy-namite act. Wish I could do that.''

"All it takes is practice," I said. "And I've had enough to know you don't just drop in to watch re-hearsals." I glanced at my watch. Time was squeezing in on me. There was so much to do and so little time to show it all to Michelle for this evening's perfor-mance.

"Don't have that much time myself, though this morning was a bit better than most," Worthington said. "I got two of my men back off administrative. One's still not worth a bucket of warm spit. He's the one that wasted the little kid.''

"Willie," I said in exasperation. "What is it?"

He looked out of the corner of his eye at Michelle, as if sizing her up. Then he said, "There's been another one. Like the other night. We need some help on it, Peter. I need you.''

"Absolutely not," I said. "I just spent the afternoon doing your work for you.''

"We turned in a con artist named Magyar," Mi-chelle said. She was rightfully proud of her part in it, but she didn't know that Worthington was a homicide detective and couldn't care less about bunco.

"Magyar? Yeah, I saw the name on the blotter. He was sprung about an hour ago.''

"What?" Michelle just stared at him.

"Why?" I asked, guessing at the reason.

Worthington shrugged. "The usual. He was spouting all sorts of stuff. He finally got around to saying some-thing that one of the narcs wanted to hear.''

"Narc? Magyar was dealing drugs?" Michelle was aghast.

"Nothing of the sort. His name was Cameron or something like that, and he was clean when it came to the hard stuff. No, he was in a position to pick up all manner of info. When he saw he had something the drug guys wanted, he started singing.''

"So you sprung him in return for the details of some drug-related crime, right?"

"Peter, you know how it works. Of course, *they* sprung him." Worthington emphasized that he or anyone he approved of wasn't responsible for this miscarriage of justice, but I knew he would have done the same if Magyar had even a whit of information needed to solve a murder. "The drug boys get the money now. Murders don't count, unless somebody important buys it or they're drug related. Whatever they say is gospel."

"That's terrible. Magyar was defrauding those people. He might have been responsible for a woman's death if he hadn't been stopped." Michelle Ferris had obviously led a sheltered existence if this shocked her. The drug dealers would sell their own grandmothers for a chance to walk—and it worked that way for other criminals, too. Anything to keep from doing time was fair game.

"So be glad he was stopped," Worthington said. To me, he said in a lower voice, "I really need your help. The same MO as before." He saw this didn't entice me. "It's developing into a serial killing. Do you want to let him keep on killing?"

I started to mention the penknife given me, but Michelle broke my train of thought.

"Peter, what's this? A murder?" Michelle looked at me with her wide eyes. I knew what she would want me to do. It wasn't that easy. If I so much as touched another anklet or belonging of one of the victims of the terrible dismemberment slayings, it might mean my sanity. I *lived* the victims' deaths. In a way, they were luckier than I was. They were dead and couldn't suffer anymore.

I kept on long after I'd dropped the bit of metal I was touching. My dreams were filled with their screams of agony. I suffered as they had—over and over and over.

"I won't, Willie. More than that, I can't. I've got to get Michelle ready for this evening's performance."

"I won't keep you long. Not more than a couple hours. That'd give you two plenty of time to work out the details."

"She's new to the biz," I said. "She needs to go through the entire act a dozen times or more before—"

"I can do it while you're gone, Peter. You told me to move from white to yellow to red and back. And you've got a list of your stunts. I can try to work through what I need to do."

"Michelle, please."

"She's on the side of law and order, Peter. She's a fine, upstanding citizen."

I felt a vicious surge. "The cops let Magyar go in return for a few details of some dope deal. Why should I work with you on this? If the suspect knows anything about drugs, the same deal will be worked. You just said as much. The DEA runs the show now, and to hell with any murders unless they're drug related."

"Peter, that's not exactly what I meant." Worthington tried to backpedal. In a way it was worth watching him try to weasel out. "I've got some clout. I've been with the department long enough to know how to play hardball in cases like this. A serial killer, Peter. That's who we're after."

I sighed. Headlines were everything now. Six o'clock news coverage. Spin doctors and media experts ran the show. Worthington could get more press off these killings than the drug agents could on even a ten-ton bust of coke. But I didn't *want* to be a part of the investigation. I truly feared for my sanity if I was embroiled in the hideous world of pain and torture I had glimpsed the night before.

"Is it . . . bad?" Michelle asked.

Worthington only nodded. I noted that he had been reticent about going into the details. It wasn't like him to skimp on such particulars out of purely social concerns. He was doing it as a lever to make me help him. It wasn't stated but it was still blackmail: if I didn't help him, he'd tell Michelle everything about the other murder.

Don't! I can't take the pain!

I gripped the edge of the table and shook.

"Are you all right, Peter? You look terrible. Sit down," Michelle said. "I'll get you a drink of water."

Sometimes the psychometry confuses the senses. I had experienced the woman's death cries as taste. An acid burning worse than any bile made me want to vomit. To drink anything now would complete the process. I motioned her off, still not able to speak. My tongue felt like a used catcher's mitt.

"Sometimes he gets like this," Worthington said. "It's nothing serious."

"But he's—"

"I'll go with you," I said to Worthington. "Michelle, there's a large green notebook in my dressing room. Get it. It details the order of the tricks and gives some indication about how I do them. Read it over. Run through the entire show several times and get the sequence of stunts into your mind."

"I'll follow the white-yellow-red when I do," she said.

"Good. I won't be long, will I?"

"Not more than an hour," Worthington promised. "I'll even stand the pair of you to dinner."

"No!" I spoke too sharply. My stomach churned and my mouth grew fuzz now from the memory of the sensation-confused psychometry. To endure whatever Willie Worthington was going to get for us was more than any human could stand.

"Why not, Peter?" Michelle asked. "I think it's a sweet offer."

"There's nothing sweet about it," I said. "The Geneva Conventions prevent mistreatment by dinner. Let's go, Willie."

He flashed a winning smile at Michelle and helped me down the short flight of stairs. By the time I reached the Rialto's lobby, I was feeling better.

"You shouldn't scare the little lady like that, Peter. It's not good for your image."

"I couldn't keep the afterimage of that woman's death from rising up," I said. "This is a bad one, Willie. Not as bad as the quartz knife was, but it's nothing I can handle if I get too involved." I had been mixed up in another murder investigation through psychometry. The murderer's emotional outpouring had been imprinted in the crystal structure of a ritual knife. Every time I touched the knife I had experienced the emotional release as an ear-splitting scream of pain.

"We'll keep it under control, Peter. You know I wouldn't want to lose your help on these cases."

"The hell you wouldn't," I said. "You'd trade your own mother for a good conviction."

"Maybe so, in this case. I don't want a serial killer thinking he can get away with it. You know they get bolder with every death."

"You're sure it's a man? I didn't get that kind of impression off the woman's anklet."

Worthington pointed to his battered black-and-white Dodge. It looked as if it had driven a hundred thousand miles on patrol, then had the SFPD insignia scraped off. We got in, the springs squeaking ominously.

"So I lost last Sunday's demolition derby," Worthington said. "It gets me from here to there."

"Why do you think the murderer's a man?"

"How many serial killers have been women? I'm playing the odds on it. The nature of the crime says it's a man. Do you disagree? Have you picked up something you're not telling me?"

"I hadn't thought about it. I suppose you're right." All I wanted to do was sit back and try to force away the burgeoning headache threatening to split my skull apart. My mouth was a disaster area and I needed peace and quiet desperately. Getting that tranquillity was akin to having Ed McMahon send me ten million dollars.

"So tell me about it," I said tiredly. "Another woman?"

"A man this time. Other than that change, the corpse is in about the same condition. We've got half a man to work with—the bottom half. If we hadn't fished the woman out of the Bay, I'd've made him the way I wanted to on the other: a jumper who had gotten caught in some ship's propeller.''

"Any differences?"

"Not worth mentioning." Worthington chewed on his lower lip for a bit before adding, "There might be one big difference. This one's still got his pants on."

"The body's clothed?" Somehow this surprised me. I wasn't sure why it should have.

"Leastwise, he's got his drawers on. There weren't any shoes or socks."

I sat back in the seat and stared ahead. There was a thought struggling to come to the surface of my mind but everytime I tried coaxing it to usefulness, a wisp of memory would obliterate it. The power of the psychometry robbed me of all rational thought. I was reduced to a quivering blob of undifferentiated protoplasm because of the stark terror the woman had felt before dying.

"Doesn't mean much, I know," Worthington said after a few minutes. "The woman might have lost her clothing during her stint in the Bay. Damned weird things in those currents."

"Maybe there was a kinky shark," I said.

Worthington drove expertly through the traffic, getting us to the Bay in record time. We weren't a dozen yards from where the other body had washed up.

Worthington's partner, Burnside, opened the door for me. I got out in a daze. I wasn't looking forward to what I would be expected to do.

"So you fetched the trained animal?" Burnside said sarcastically.

I stared at him as if he were a lower life form. In some ways, he was. Not even Worthington could put up with him on a daily basis and think Burnside and humanity had much in common.

"Animal trainer," I corrected. "Go roll over and play dead."

"Thorne, you got a—"

"Can it, Burnside," Worthington said. "We've got to make this quick. Thorne's got to get back to the theater for a show tonight."

"Why not sell tickets here?" Burnside almost sneered. "I never seen a better performance than the one he puts on. What gets me is that you lap it up like a cat goes after cream."

"Notice all the animal references?" I asked. "Makes you wonder what he does in his spare time. What's the statute about molesting small furry animals?"

"I ought to—"

"I said to can it," Worthington said. He pushed his partner out of the way. When Burnside insisted on making a scene, Worthington took him to one side and spoke to him for several minutes. Burnside didn't cool off, but he did go away.

"I hope you didn't send him to the zoo. There won't be a safe animal in the place."

"Burnie's okay. He just doesn't believe you really *do* anything."

"Listen to him. Let me go back to work."

"I believe you have a talent. I'm not convinced it's what you say. Psychometry is a bit farfetched, even in a world with neutrinos and black holes and shit like that. Whatever you do, it helps me catch the bad guys. That's what's important."

"Let's get this over." I was in no condition to psychometrize, but the sooner I got to work, the sooner I'd be able to recuperate. I needed to be one hundred percent for the show tonight. A new assistant is always worrisome, even when she was as quick on the uptake as Michelle Ferris seemed to be.

"Weird how both bodies came to the surface in about the same area. That's got to be a fluke," Worthington was saying as he walked along. He had pulled out his yellow stub of a pencil and scribbled constantly in his spiral notebook. He recorded everything he saw and heard and thought against the day he went to court.

"Have you checked the currents?" I asked. "There might be some way of figuring out where the bodies went into the Bay."

"That's not too likely. The ME figures the first body was in the drink for a couple weeks. There's been a bad storm in that time that mixed up the Bay currents. You remember it last week. Nasty rain and cold wind for two days. Even if this one went in at the same time as the first body, the likelihood of it coming up now, at almost the same place as the other, is pure chance."

I wished there were some way of tracking the course of the two bodies. I had the gut feeling that the murderer had thrown both corpses into the Bay at the same place, if not the same time. In a way, it only made sense. People see the damnedest things. The murderer had to have a safe spot to unload a car trunk and throw the body in.

I rubbed my eyes. This was only speculation. The murderer might own a boat. A leisurely sunset sail, wait a while until it was too dark for anyone to notice what was happening, slide the body overboard. It was quick and easy.

"Why not sail out beyond the Golden Gate Bridge?" I asked aloud.

"What's that?" Worthington looked at me as if I had grown horns and a forked tail.

"I had the thought that the murderer needed a secluded spot to dump the bodies so he wouldn't be seen driving up and unloading them. Then I thought he might have a boat, but if he did, why not go out to sea a mile or two before dumping the bodies?"

"A good point. We've got men canvassing the Embarcadero trying to turn something up, but the same thought occurred to me. If you've got the boat, use it. Don't futz around in the Bay to unload your victims. A tour boat full of tourists would get you on videotape every time."

I had to walk carefully to keep from losing my balance on the slippery stones paving the bank leading down to the shoreline. They were intended to prevent erosion. So far as I could see, all they prevented was an easy climb back up.

At the bottom I stood on a sandy spit, staring up at the blackness of the Golden Gate Bridge's underside. The shadows were like ink and cast a pall over the entire area. I wondered if the murderer dumped his victims off the bridge or brought them here and left them. That thought vanished as quickly as it came. No one did anything private on the Golden Gate Bridge. Jumpers were spotted quickly these days. Stopping in a car created a traffic jam. And both bodies had been in the water for more than a week.

Floaters, the police called them.

"Here he is," Worthington said. He pulled back an opaque black plastic shroud. Even though I thought I was prepared for the sight, I wasn't.

"You never get used to it," Worthington said, not showing any sign that the sight of half a man bothered him. "The clothing's ruined but there's a belt buckle you might be able to psychometrize."

"Is there anything else?" I asked. I didn't want to look at the middle of the torso that had been hacked away. The fish had done a good job of cleaning out the guts, but the gaping cavity made me want to lose my meager breakfast. After the woman's body yesterday, I wasn't getting much in the way of food.

"Nothing else that looks as promising," Worthington said. "The forensics team has done everything but X-ray the remains. The belt buckle's the only hunk of metal on the body."

"Can you put it into a plastic bag so I won't get my fingerprints on it?"

"No problem, Peter. Forensics did that at my request." Worthington picked up the small bag. I hadn't seen it beside the body. I was too fixated on the half corpse. "They think I'm strange in what I ask for, but I've got a good track record. That's what counts."

Worthington stood holding the bag. His usually jovial expression faded as he handed me the buckle. "This is important, Peter. The first body we kept from the press. This one's got to be released. We can't have more piling up on us without all kinds of shit falling from the sky."

"I understand," I said. "I hope I'm not your only lead."

When he didn't answer, I knew that I was. This put even more pressure on me. I settled down on my heels and closed my eyes. Controlling my breathing, letting soft breezes blow across my face and mind, I tried to relax and put my concerns aside. I had trained myself enough that I was able to go into a light meditative state. It might not be enough to properly psychometrize, but if the psychic imprint on the buckle was as strong as on the anklet, the shallow state would be enough.

Floating, drifting through my own mind, I reached out and took the buckle. My fingers rested lightly on it, not feeling the plastic, not even feeling the cold metal. I sought the deeper resonances left by a living, breathing person.

Even as I tentatively walked out on the astral plane where I might find these vibrations and decipher their sense-confusing message, I knew I had failed. Settling into a deeper trance did no good.

I opened my eyes and blinked to focus.

"Well, Peter, what did you get?" Worthington's eagerness for an answer was almost pathetic. It more than anything else told the despair he was facing in this case. He wasn't having any luck turning up clues on his own.

His face fell when he saw that I had come up empty. "I'm sorry," I said. "The buckle is new. The man hadn't worn it long enough for me to get any kind of reading from it."

Willie Worthington turned and walked off without a word. I put the bag with its lonely contents back on the ground and tried not to look at the body again, then followed Worthington back to his car. He drove me to the Rialto in stony silence.

Somehow, I felt worse failing Willie than if I had relived the victim's death.

CHAPTER 7

"You look like something the cat dragged in," Michelle said, glancing up from the green three-ring notebook containing all my tricks. I dropped into an uncomfortable chair at the corner of my dressing room and just sat, staring into space.

"Peter? Are you all right?"

"I'm fine," I said. "How's the rehearsal coming? I didn't mean to be so long, but Worthington's little investigation was more complicated than I'd thought." This wasn't true. Not being able to psychometrize the dead man's belt buckle had cut a considerable portion of time off the trip. It still worried me that I had been unable to get any information off the buckle for Worthington. He had looked so crestfallen that he might fly off the handle when he had to talk with the press.

There wasn't any doubt in my mind now that his time had come. One murder victim pulled from the Bay wasn't much in the way of news. The condition of the body was gruesome but the jumper/ship's propeller theory covered the facts. Two bodies in identical condition strained at coincidence. The more the coroner worked over the bodies the more proof there would be that the victims first had been tortured and then dismembered. This was the stuff that sold papers for weeks—or until the killer was caught.

I knew personally there was damned near nothing for the police to work on. Most murders are solved within ten days. If there isn't a significant break in the case by then, it's pushed aside into an open but inactive file. The detective in charge might not like it but that's the way the world works. Worthington had been complaining about a rush of murders and a dearth of officers to investigate. With a crime like this, the usual police tactic was to assign more and more men to go out and pound the pavement until a clue was dredged up. Such a marshaling of manpower for a single case couldn't last long. Even in the most famous ones, there hadn't been an army of officers working for longer than a month.

Time—and crime—marched on. New victims would be found with a better chance of putting their killers into jail. The police had to play the odds. If they wanted to get even a small portion of the murderers off the streets, they had to go with what experience told them was the best way to work. A man cutting people in half wasn't going to simply go away, but if he didn't try it again, in a month or two Willie Worthington might find himself the only detective on the case.

Having a man capable of such a ghastly crime loose to do it again in a year or five made my stomach churn.

"You don't look too good, Peter," Michelle repeated. "Is it the idea of having a green assistant?"

"No, it's not you," I assured her. "It's the case Worthington wanted me to help on. It . . . bothers me."

"It didn't sound as if it was a nice clean bust like Magyar," she said.

I shook it off. I hadn't lost myself in the strange world of psychometry and didn't have to fight off the fresh effects of the sense-twisting flight into the mind of someone who had been tortured and cut in half. That was small consolation. It might have been better if I could've psychometrized and caught the son of bitch. A missed performance was nothing in comparison to a feat like that.

"Tell me about yourself," I said to change the subject. "Why did you come to San Francisco? There's nothing here for a dancer." I didn't mention the places along Columbus Avenue where nude dancers worked. Michelle wasn't up for that kind of work, and her aunt had been specific about the costume or lack of it Michelle was to wear.

I watched as Michelle blushed. She dropped her eyes and mumbled something I didn't hear. I've learned an interrogation technique from watching Worthington with his low-life felons. Say nothing and the subject will try to fill the void.

"I wasn't exactly a dancer," she said. "I got mixed up with some rough trade."

I laughed. "Out here, the term 'rough trade' obviously doesn't mean what it does back East." I clamped my mouth shut when she turned those blue, blue eyes on me.

"It does. I was working in porno movies. I moved in with the director of one of the flicks and he . . . he started renting me out."

"He was your pimp?"

"You might call it that. I didn't get anything from him except abuse and a few broken bones. When Aunt Gloria heard that I was in one of his skin flicks, she hit the ceiling."

"What about your parents?"

Michelle shrugged in a way I've come to associate with the thirteen-year-old hookers along Polk. It said nothing and everything.

"I'm sorry. This is none of my business."

"I want to tell you, Peter. You've been so kind to me. And this afternoon, actually arresting Magyar was a real kick. They *can* be sent up. Crooks, I mean."

"You heard Worthington. There's not much chance Magyar will do time. He's probably already out of the city."

"That's all right. You stopped him from harming anyone." Michelle straightened. "*We* stopped him."

"I suppose." I was doubtful about how much good we had really done. If anything, we had averted future misery and death, but probably not by much. Anyone who is desperate enough to fall for Magyar's pitch would seek out another faith healer and go right back into the same hole.

"I wasn't with him for long," she said, abruptly switching back to her life story. "I wasn't old enough to understand what I was getting into."

"How long?" Sticking my nose into Michelle's private life was foolish, but I heard a faint quiver in her voice saying she needed to tell someone. She'd kept a lot bottled up and it was time to let it come rushing out.

"Four films. We shot one a week. And when he started charging his S&M friends to use me, that's when I got up the nerve to leave him. He was so different after I moved in."

"It seemed innocent enough and why the hell not?" I asked.

"Something like that. I did want to be in show business. He persuaded me this was a good way to start. It didn't hurt Marilyn Chambers's career any."

"Such as it is. I saw *Rabid* and it was hardly a high-budget flick. I don't remember her ever being in anything else that wasn't a porn movie, except maybe *Party Incorporated* and one or two others."

"She made a lot of money off her film career."

I had no idea about that. She had started in San Francisco with the Mitchell Brothers. They were probably as honest as anyone in the movie business. Again, I wasn't sure if that said much. For all I knew they were princes among men and made the real movie moguls look like robber barons.

"So you left and came out here?"

"Not right away. I had to go into the hospital first. I was pretty badly banged up. I've still got a few scars, but the bones have mended. Aunt Gloria didn't seem to care. If anything, she understood. I spent some time in another kind of hospital, too." The way she said it, Michelle thought this was worse than letting her pimp beat her up. If the shrink had helped set her back to a more even keel, where was the disgrace? But society was odd that way. Any physical problem was expected to be patched up just fine. If anything, scars were a badge of courage and honor. But going to a psychiatrist ruined political careers and made ordinary people uptight.

"She's a bit overprotective, but otherwise I'd never have guessed that anything was out of the ordinary. Have you ever been onstage?"

"Not in front of a live crowd. But after working on those horrible movies, I can do about anything, Peter. I'm sure of it. You can't imagine what it's like having a dozen dirty old men wheezing and laughing and making lewd suggestions while you're—" Michelle stopped and swallowed hard as memories rushed back.

Again, I had no idea what she had been through. I only shook my head. Saying I understood would have been a lie, just as much as her saying she understood what I felt when I psychometrized the dead woman's anklet.

"I can do it. I know I can. I've been working all afternoon on memorizing the book."

"Let's do a quick run-through of the entire act. We've got time. Then we can break for dinner and get back in time for the show."

"I've got what I have to do memorized. There won't be any problem tonight. I promise."

"Don't concern yourself about that. There are almost always problems, no matter how many times you've gone through an act. It's up to me to cover the fumbles, miscues, and the outright gaffes. That's what I get paid for. Now let's rehearse."

The run-through went better than it had any right to. I made a few minor changes but saw that the show would go on. It might not be my best, but it would be a world better than last night's show with Julianne's attention drifting away to wherever her boyfriend was.

"It's going great," I said. "You haven't missed a cue yet."

"Thanks, Peter. I'm still nervous. I thought it was supposed to go away after a few minutes."

"The jitters never really go away. That's all right. It gives a sharp edge to your performance." I waited as the stagehands cleared the apparatus from the last trick and set up the small table with the lion cub in it. I didn't want to do the pigeons into lion bit, but Barry Morgan had insisted. He had come in to watch just as Michelle and I were finishing our rehearsal.

"Time to go forth again and smile a lot." Michelle wiggled out onto the stage and prepared the audience for the transmutation act.

I followed a beat later and began the trick. The trap-door refused to yield, and I ended up having to force it. The spring snapped and the lion burst out. Only my quick reflexes saved us having to chase the feisty little monster into the audience. I grabbed the cub by the scruff of its neck and held him aloft to thunderous applause. They hadn't seen how I had slid my fingers into the half-open slit and pried it open. Best of all, Michelle had moved just enough to hide the pigeons vanishing into their small compartment. For a split second, all three animals were in view.

I took the lion cub offstage and dumped him into a wire cage vowing to never again work with such unmanageable creatures—and that included the Rialto's manager. But this was only an excuse for my uneasiness. Something was happening and I couldn't put my finger on it. It was a tough house to work tonight, but that was nothing new. The Rialto didn't always draw the best there was in way of clientele.

Something more gnawed away as I worked. Trying to look out over the house wasn't too productive, either, since I needed my full concentration for the act. Michelle was working out well, but occasional hesitations on her part threw my timing subtly off. It wasn't anything I hadn't anticipated. So what was bugging me? There didn't seem to be any way of answering that. I put it off to the stage jitters I'd warned Michelle about.

Returning to the stage, I intoned, "For the finale I shall perform my world famous mind-reading act. My assistant shall pass among you and gather a few odds and ends. Securely blindfolded, I shall endeavor to reveal your inner self from the quantum mechanical vibrations inherent in all matter."

I wasn't going to psychometrize any of the knick-knacks she selected. Michelle had learned the list of twenty key words. When she uttered these seemingly innocent words, she communicated a great deal to me about the owner of the artifact. The first few wouldn't be "readable" because she would be feeding me information about the third and fourth items. This built up the tension and made the audience think I wasn't able to give a decent reading. It made it all the more startling when I began hitting exact details.

The lighting director again earned my eternal thanks. He kept the bright ellipsoid on Michelle and hit me with a medium scarlet that made it appear that my head was aglow.

The first two items were complete washouts, as we had planned. I had a good deal of information by the time we reached the third selection Michelle had made, a wristwatch. She held it up behind my head.

"The man—no, the woman—who owns this is short, not even five feet tall," I said. "It does not keep good time. It is running slow, no, not slow. It is set for Eastern time. The owner of the watch is from New York City."

The latter wasn't as difficult a guess as it might have been. The woman must have said a few words to Michelle, who recognized the accent and fed me the line.

An amazed gasp went up from the audience and a woman said in a heavy Brooklyn accent, "That's amazing. How'd ya know that?"

"The cosmic vibrations are everywhere. I have trained myself to intercept and interpret them," I said pompously. From somewhere in the back of the theater came a baritone laugh. A nonbeliever. I almost wanted to assure him he was right.

"The next item, please," I said, already knowing Michelle held up a tie bar over my head.

I started to go over the information from the code words she had given me when I stopped. I groped over my head and said, "Hand it to me. I need to touch the tie bar."

I tried to salvage something from the act by identifying the object. The instant I took it, I reeled. Settling myself, I began to really psychometrize. My hands shook as I held the tie bar.

Not my hands. Don't hurt my hands. Aieee!

I shook like a leaf in a high wind. The voice speaking in my head, the imprint from the tie bar, was identical to the owner of the penknife. The deeper into my trance I went the more confused the impressions became. My senses twisted what I was experiencing.

I heard taste. I saw feel. And I smelled fear.

Take the chains off my feet! Don't swing me. Not over that! Not upside down!

Sweat beaded my brow and soaked into the folds of the black silk blindfold. The tie clip slipped from my nerveless fingers as pain shot into my forearms and shoulders. I was being pulled aloft, my feet tied together. Blood ran down my elbows as I swung to and fro.

Over huge scissors that opened and snapped shut. The image shifted constantly, mixing sight and smell and feel in a mad welter I couldn't understand. Fear caused my heart to contract and miss a beat. Pain ravaged my torso as skin peeled away and blood flowed. Then I was spun in wild circles, my senses totally out of control.

I hit the floor hard and heard voices above me. I tried to fight as I came out of my trance. My arms thrashed about weakly.

"Peter!" My name echoed and tasted like blood. "Peter, sit up. You're onstage. Please!"

I ripped off the blindfold and obeyed the voice. I blinked hard, the lights in my eyes. Michelle held my arm. I pulled away, not wanting to get my blood on her. It took a few seconds for me to realize I was unscathed. My physical body was untouched; only my psychic one had endured the injuries—shared the injuries to my arms and head.

"Whose tie clip is this?" I said, struggling to stand. I held it up so that the light caught it and reflected brightly. There was deathly silence in the audience. "Please tell me. Whose is this? I'd like to explore other objects from this person."

There was no response from the audience. I asked Michelle out of the corner of my mouth, "Who gave it to you? Whose is it?"

"A man in the fourth row. That one," she said, pointing.

"Sir, is this yours?"

The man looked around, as if thinking I spoke to someone near him. He finally said, "That's not mine. It was passed down to the aisle. It belongs to somebody else."

The empty seats in both the fourth and fifth rows told me whoever had sent this to Michelle was probably long gone.

The echoing deep bass laughter from the rear of the theater chilled me more than any arctic storm wind.

"Thank you," I said, bowing slightly. "You have been a good audience."

The applause was light, most of them not knowing what to make of my peculiar behavior. I made a beeline to the pay phone at the rear of the theater. Michelle stopped me before I could dial.

"What happened, Peter? You scared me!"

"I've got to call Worthington. The tie clip. It belongs to the same man."

"What man?" she demanded. "What's going on?"

"The tie bar and the penknife belong to the same man," I said. "And he died."

Scissors snapped shut under me. I winced, then turned and placed the call. Whoever sent me the knife and tie clip had killed their owner. But why was he tormenting me by allowing me to psychometrize them?

CHAPTER 8

"I'm sorry, Peter. It was awful what I did. I shouldn't have done it."

"Don't bother apologizing anymore, Michelle. You're making me feel guilty." She kept on harping about last night's performance and accepting the tie clip without seeing who had passed it to her.

"I'm the one who's to blame, Peter. I wouldn't blame you if you fired me."

The way she looked at me with such expectation made me wonder about her motives. Did she want to quit? If so, she could just come out and say it. On the other hand, she had enjoyed the performance, alternating between ordinary stage fright and real eagerness to be in front of the audience. That was the balancing act most successful performers go through all the time.

"You did fine," I said, putting my arms around her and holding her for a moment. "It takes a while to learn all the tricks. A really good magician's assistant needs more than a year onstage to learn everything. If it were easy, everyone would be doing it."

I made a large coin appear in my hand. I began running it up and down my fingers to show my dexterity. I moved my hand so that the palm faced Michelle and did the same trick. This time it looked as if the coin vanished from under my hand and magically appeared on top. A slight variation caused the coin to poke out a milled rim between any two fingers I wanted.

"That took me six weeks of hard practice to learn. I dropped the coin more times than I got it from one side to the other, but now it's second nature and I can concentrate on other things while I'm doing it. It's like that with everything. You did fine and you'll keep getting better. I've got confidence in you.''

''Wh-what I said about my background doesn't bother you?''

''No.'' This was another attempt to put herself down. Michelle was working up to claiming she wasn't worthy of this job because of her lousy choice in men.

''Thank you, Peter. You're everything Aunt Gloria said—and more.''

''Let's get on with the payoff,'' I said. We were just outside the Gadsen Gallery, almost an hour early for Gloria's reception for her new artistic discovery. ''We'll look the place over, make sure we know where all the mirrors are, then—''

''Mirrors?''

''I never work with a mirror to one side or behind me. It lets the audience see what's really going on.'' I cleared my throat. ''That is, I never work with a mirror unless that's where I want them to look. In a party atmosphere like this, all we need are a couple corners to keep people from getting behind me.''

''I ought to run interference if they try?''

''See?'' I said. ''You catch on fast. Now let's see if Gloria's got some hors de'oeuvres out. I'm starved.''

We went down the stairs to the gallery's lower level. The same receptionist I had seen before glanced up. She flashed a quick smile at Michelle and pretty well ignored me. I must not have been on the ''A'' list.

''Is my aunt upstairs, Marie?''

''Yes, ma'am, she went up to do some bookkeeping about an hour ago. You just run on up. I'm sure she'll want to see you before the place fills up.''

''We won't be a minute,'' Michelle said. She spiraled up the wrought-iron staircase. I followed, dragging along my case with many of the tricks I would be performing throughout the evening. I'd need at least a half hour to put everything away and prepare the stunts.

''Michelle!'' cried Gloria Gadsen. ''How did the

show go? I didn't read anything in the paper about the stage being rushed by an angry mob last night.''

"It went okay," Michelle said reluctantly.

"The performance was better than I could have hoped, Gloria," I said. "Your niece is too modest. She did great. With some practice working together, we're going to be a dynamite team.''

"You're willing to keep her on? You don't have someone with more experience lined up?''

"You're too paranoid. Michelle can keep working with me, if she wants. All I ask is a two-week notice if she wants to quit. It's hell trying to get a last-minute replacement. I think I probably used up all my luck finding her.''

Michelle smiled and the room brightened. Her mood swings were more evident now that I had been around her for a day. As long as she worked well with me, that would help her self-image. I let out a small sigh as I thought of some of the assistants I'd worked with. Compared to them Michelle was a pro.

"Good, glad to hear the show went so well," Gloria said. "Do you need somewhere to change?''

"There's no need for costumes," I said. "I do need to get loaded up, though. This coat's filled with pockets for all my gimmicks. I'd prefer if only Michelle watched.''

"Trade secrets, I know," Gloria said. "We'll get you a back room you can use. The press and the other invited guests won't show up for at least an hour.''

"Could we mooch some food, Aunt Gloria? Peter hasn't eaten, and I'm a bit hungry myself.''

"I don't want to eat or drink anything after we begin," I said. "I have to be sure my fingers are absolutely clean for some of my coin manipulations.'' To show her I repeated the trick I'd shown Michelle earlier. The coins raced back and forth in my dexterous fingers. It was impressive enough to illustrate my point and helped me get my coordination and motility up to par.

"Nice," Gloria said. "That's the kind of stunt I was hoping you'd do to amuse them. They are such a jaded group. Go tell Marie to set you up in a back room and have her fetch you some food and anything you want to drink?"

"Nothing alcoholic for me," I said.

"There'll be plenty of that horrible fizzy water. Art critics don't drink anything else, at least in public. I think it makes their noses wrinkle up just the right amount so they can sneer at everything they see," Gloria said. She was already going back to her stacks of receipts and record books. I indicated to Michelle that we ought to be starting our preparations.

Marie found some small sandwiches with the crusts cut off. It was hardly my idea of a meal, but I had been too busy to eat anything today. Last night's performance had taken a great deal out of me. I had tried to call Willie Worthington and tell him that someone had sent through the audience a man's penknife and tie bar that might figure into a murder. The image of the scissors snipping kept returning to haunt me, blotting out even the images from the woman's anklet.

The small storeroom Marie showed us was filled with the odors of oil and paint thinner, of dust and other oddities found in an art gallery. I ignored them and began secreting the various contraptions in coattails, hidden pockets, and even up the sleeve. A good magician can work items in and out of the sleeves and no one will be the wiser. It's even easier if you push the sleeve up first to show you don't have anything there. That simple motion can either retrieve or insert enough gadgetry for several tricks.

"You must clank when you walk," Michelle said, dismayed by the amount of stuff I managed to hide on me.

"Part of the act is not clanking," I said, my mind anticipating the tricks, trying to figure out the best places for them.

"The first of the guests are coming in," Michelle

said, looking out the door. "What are we supposed to do?"

"Greet them. Be pleasant and don't show any reaction, no matter what I do. There's not much you can do except act as my shill. I might feed you straight lines. Reply so that it moves me into the trick."

"But I don't know what you'll want to do next," she protested.

"You saw what I hid. Alternate between them. I might even take my cues from what you say or do."

"But, Peter—"

"Let's mingle," I said. The truth was there was little need for Michelle to act as my assistant this evening. This was going to be ad-lib all the way.

I went out and started scouting likely places to perform. As I made my slow circuit of the gallery, I got my first good look at Gloria's budding artist's work. It didn't impress me too much. For the most part, it looked as if he had just tossed paint onto a canvas and then hung some sexy name on it that had no bearing to reality.

"Nonobjectivist art," came a high-pitched voice behind me. "Are you a collector?"

"An interested guest," I said. The man had a press pass stuck in his pocket where everyone was sure to notice. He had to be an art critic. "What do you think of Mr. Taggart's work?"

"Taggart, he wants to be known only as Taggart. I personally find it overwhelming. I find great power and scope in his conception. You see this one? Note the strong lines, followed by the prodigious arc that changes color?"

I saw what the man pointed out, but it meant nothing to me other than smears of paint. We walked along. Most of Taggart's pieces were uninvolving. Then I came to one and just stared. "This one," I said. "There's a power in it that's not in the others. It's almost as if I can feel it."

"Yes, yes, that's it. You feel what I do about his

work. A palpable force emanates from the very canvas," the critic said, growing more excited as he spoke. "This is one of the best in the entire brilliant collection. There are flashes of genius in the other pieces. This one is *pure* genius."

I stared at the painting and wondered what affected me so strongly about it. Outwardly it wasn't much different from the others. Without thinking, I reached out to touch the painting. A powerful hand closed around my wrist and jerked me away.

"Don't get your sticky fingerprints on the artwork," growled a burly man with flame red hair. He shoved me back hard. Only luck kept me from stumbling and falling.

"Sorry," I said. "There was something about this piece that drew me. I know better."

"Bloody well right, you ought to know better, you dumb fucker."

The man's insult made me stiffen. It was out of proportion to my momentary indiscretion.

"I said I was sorry. Now you can apologize to me for being so rude."

"Fuck off." The man shoved me again and stormed off, his waffle-stomper boots smacking hard against the gallery's wooden floor.

"Peter, wait," called out Gloria Gadsen. She rushed over, her hand fluttering to her throat. "Don't get him mad. He's such a bear! I warned you about him."

"He's—" I stopped and counted to five to get my anger in check. Then I said, "That's your pet artist, isn't it?"

"Taggart, yes," she said. "I said he carried the angry young man shtick a bit too far. He thinks it will sell paintings."

I looked back at the one that had so captivated me. "What is it about this one?"

Gloria just shrugged. "They're all pretty much the same. You see the same color scheme? That's his trademark."

"There is a certain continuity in color," I said. "Did he mix one color in with all the others?"

"That's common practice to prevent counterfeiting," Gloria said. "Rembrandt did it, Vermeer did it." She smiled crookedly. "If Taggart ever found out that Vermeer crushed up rubies and emeralds and mixed that in with his paint, he'd insist on doing it, too."

"Precious gems?"

"It increased the value of the painting. It also played hob with the paint. The dust remained long after the paint flaked off and gave a grainy, uneven texture that never restored well. Some of the artists selling to the Medicis mixed varnish in with their paint. The varnish cracked and changed color and ruined the work after a few decades." Gloria Gadsen looked at Taggart's paintings. "I hope he's not doing something stupid like that. The last thing I need is a complaint about his materials."

"Jackson Pollock's work was made to fall apart," I said. "He thought it increased its value."

"I'm worried about Taggart decreasing his. Excuse me, Peter. He's picking another fight with Jason. Oh, Jason, darling, how are you?" Gloria Gadsen went rushing off to pacify the art critic I had spoken with earlier. It didn't make any sense for Taggart to antagonize the man; he had liked the work and would undoubtedly give it a top review.

I shook my head. Taggart wasn't likely to do anything like a normal person. He had his own ideas on how to attract attention. Rather than letting his work speak for itself, he bellowed and roared and insulted to create a form of gonzo art. Still, as I walked off, I had to look over my shoulder at the painting—*Maelstrom of Disquiet.*

It *was* disquieting.

Gloria had taken Taggart to one side and was reading him the riot act. His florid face got redder by the minute, but she had him back in control. His huge hands were balled into tight fists but he didn't look as if he'd start swinging anytime soon. To distract the guests from the little psychodrama being played out, I began work.

At first, I didn't have anyone watching me, but Michelle came over and acted as the shill I needed. In a few minutes everyone watched as I manipulated cards and did small sleight-of-hand tricks. I pulled lighted cigarettes from thin air, apologized for smoking, and swallowed the lit cigarette. I did the three-coin vanish and reappearance and then ended with an amusing little trick.

I held up the jack of hearts from a deck of cards, showing it front and back. I placed it faceup on the wood floor, then stepped on it. I moved away without looking down.

"It changed!" came the amazed observation from the woman next to Michelle. "How'd you do that?"

"Magic," I said softly, taking a quick bow.

"Not so fast." The woman picked up the card and looked at it carefully. It was just a playing card and nothing more. Michelle rescued the card from the woman, and we made our way through the crowd, speaking to a few of the people, accepting congratulations and even a pat on the back from Jason the art critic.

"How'd you do that one?" asked Michelle, almost breathless. "That was great!"

"And so simple," I said. When no one was looking, I peeled the jack of hearts off my shoe sole where it had been stuck with a bit of wax. "I held up two cards for examination, put both down, then just picked up the top one, leaving the other."

"That's so simple."

"That's magic," I said. I saw that we didn't have to perform anymore. Gloria had Taggart seated at the side of the gallery and tapped on a water glass to get everyone's attention.

I had my first chance to see the people Gloria had invited. Most had the appearance of patrons of the arts, well dressed and slightly snooty looking. Several scribbled notes for reviews. Two men I recognized from newspaper articles.

As luck would have it, one came over for a better view as Gloria started detailing the more arcane points of Taggart's work.

"Move, will you?" the man said, elbowing me aside. "I want to get a look at the yokel's work."

I stepped back. If Taggart had a buyer, more power to him. It seemed as if Taggart and the man—Clarke Yancey—deserved each other's company.

"I make fifty-eight million a year," Yancey said. I suppose he was talking to me since there wasn't anyone else nearby except for Michelle and the man at Yancey's elbow. "Why shouldn't I spend some of it on geek art?"

"If you don't like it, why buy it?" asked Michelle.

He turned a withering look on her. She wilted like a flower in front of a blast furnace. Yancey looked over at me. "That was some stuff you did. You ought to go onstage with it."

"I do an act professionally," I said, not trusting myself to say anything more. I indicated to Michelle that we ought to move on. Yancey didn't budge, blocking my way.

"You're okay, but not that good." He spun and shouted, "I'll buy that one for a hundred grand."

"That's one way of spending your fifty million," I said. "I'm sure Taggart will want to thank you."

"One-fifty," Yancey called. "I can use it as a drop cloth when I change my oil!" He found this uproariously funny.

Taggart didn't. He came boiling out of his chair and started for Yancey. Gloria intercepted Taggart; I found myself standing between the artist and Yancey.

"Outta my way," he said, shoving me aside. I'd had enough being pushed around for the day. My mental condition was twisted and crazy with images from Worthington's first murder victim and the penknife and tie clip I'd been given during my performances.

I caught Yancey's wrist and elbow and straightened just fast enough to give him a snap of pain.

He pulled back and cocked his fist, ready to fight. The man behind him stepped between us and said, "It's not worth it, Clarke. Who is he? Just a hired performer."

"Thanks," I said. "I didn't want to hurt him."

"Don't flatter yourself," the man said. "I'm his lawyer. It's not worth taking you to court over assault and battery charges."

"But he shoved Peter first . . ." Michelle started.

"Fuck off, bitch," snarled Yancey. "Nobody asked you to butt in."

Gloria turned over the presentation to her assistant and came over when she saw the problems forming. "Mr. Pickering, let me speak to him. I'm sorry if there was any problem."

"Get him the fuck away from me," snapped Yancey.

"With pleasure," I said. I trailed Gloria to the back room where I had prepared for the small magic show.

"Peter, I'm so sorry," she said. "I expected Taggart to be difficult. I didn't think Yancey would show up. He is *so* disagreeable."

"Who is he?" asked Michelle.

"Clarke Yancey's an industrialist, though that's a polite term for what he really does," I said. "He's been up on conspiracy charges just about every year I can remember. He's got underworld ties."

"The same can be said of his lawyer, Roy Pickering," Gloria said, "but they do have money and Taggart needs it."

"I understand, Gloria. The show went well enough up to that point. Michelle and I worked together like old hands."

"Thank you, Peter. I'm not running you off, but I thought it might be better if you were out of sight for a few minutes. When everyone cools off, please come back. I need someone who's got a civil tongue in his head to be out there."

"Maybe we'd better leave," I suggested. Continuing didn't seem to be a very good idea.

"Nonsense. I want Michelle to see more of the workings of the gallery. She's not going to be a stage magician's assistant forever. And I want *you* to stay, Peter. Don't let them run you off."

Against my better judgment, I let Gloria talk me into staying and putting on another small show after the initial presentation of Taggart's paintings.

"I'd better go back and see if Marie needs help. The least Yancey can do after being so ill-mannered is to actually buy the piece. Imagine, he acted as if this were some flea market auction. The very idea."

Gloria Gadsen left, shaking her head. I let out my pent-up breath and sank to the nearest crate for a rest. I'd earned it by putting up with a couple of truly objectionable sons of bitches.

CHAPTER 9

"We ought to leave," I said. I took out most of the magic tricks I'd hidden in my coat and pants. There wouldn't be much call for more of the magic act after this fiasco.

"Please, Peter, this means so much to my aunt. She's not doing all that well with the gallery, you know. She has to sell most of Taggart's paintings or she might not even be able to meet the rent this month."

"I didn't know. Gloria's never said anything."

Michelle nodded and looked embarrassed, as if she was telling tales out of school. "She wouldn't, but I overheard her talking with Marie. They need this showing to be a success as much as Taggart does. No one's been buying any artwork."

"That's why she put up with Clarke Yancey and his obnoxious lawyer," I said. "That explains a lot. Gloria's not the kind to tolerate rudeness. Usually."

"You probably know her better than I do, but she's about all the family I have left. I want to please her."

"All right," I said tiredly. "I'd only go home and try to work out new sequences for the act. Why not mingle and try to enjoy the display?"

"Thank you, Peter." Michelle squeezed my arm, then hurried out of the storeroom. I settled my clothing, noting how wrinkles appeared when I wasn't fully laden with all the magic paraphernalia. Although it might be possible to eliminate the poor hang of the suit, I wasn't sure it was to my advantage. Better that I looked natty before the act. During it, as the wrinkles appeared and the various items were taken away, no one was likely to notice.

First impressions and all that.

I sucked in my breath and let it out slowly to settle myself when I saw that Yancey and Roy Pickering were still in the gallery. There hadn't been any need for the man to pick a fight the way he had. The only reason I could think that he had done it was to become the center of attention. I had worked the crowd and been the focus of their admiration for a few brief minutes. Yancey tried to muscle in on this fleeting notoriety.

Avoiding him, I went to the rear of the gallery and stood in front of *Maelstrom of Disquiet* once more. The painting wrenched at my emotions, and I couldn't say why. At first glance, it was no different from any of the other randomly paint-splotched canvases Taggart had hung in the gallery. Still, something spoke to me from this one and it was in a somber, almost menacing voice.

"It's markedly different from the others he's done, isn't it?" came a soft voice.

I looked over my shoulder. A nondescript woman stood just behind me, also admiring Taggart's work. She was dressed in Goodwill reject clothing, no attempt made to fit her slender form or even fix the picks and tears in the material. She had a battered tooled leather handbag slung across her body like a Mexican bandit's bandolier and wore a small red button with bold white lettering proclaiming: THIS IS NOT A FASHION STATEMENT, I AM A STREET PERSON.

"Are you one of the art critics?" I asked.

She shrugged, saying everything and nothing with the gesture. "This one is different from most of the others. I'm not a real fan of Taggart's work. He's far too pretentious for me, but this one—and that one back there. It's got the same sensation of scope, of power, and stark daring."

She tossed her head slightly and sent a wild disarray of mousy brown hair around her head like a nimbus. She didn't look back to see if I trailed her or not. She just didn't care. I liked her attitude far more than the pompous Jason or the belligerent Clarke Yancey. Even more, she seemed willing to explain the appeal of the paintings to me.

"This one, *Subway to the Soul*, carries the same visual urgency as *Maelstrom*. I don't like it as much, but it is beguiling. I find it impossible to drag my eyes off it. That makes for good art, if not great art."

I stood beside the woman and saw what she meant. There was nothing in the random squishes and squirts and drops of paint that ought to make me study it, yet the painting accomplished that.

"What's the medium? I know almost nothing about nonobjectivist art, or indeed, art at all."

The woman stepped closer and examined the painting. She stepped back, her eyes never leaving the canvas. "There might be some oils in the painting. It appears to be acrylics from the brilliance and sheen of the coloration. He mixes a single color into all his hues give it a distinctive look."

"Like Rembrandt and the other masters did," I said, remembering what Gloria Gadsen had said earlier. "Taggart must not have heard that Vermeer ground up precious stones and put those in his paint."

This got the woman's attention. She turned and her eyebrows arched. Her brown eyes danced. "You know more about art history than you let on. My name's Jena Rosetti."

"Peter Thorne," I said. "The gallery owner invited me to do a few magic stunts. I'm a stage magician."

"I'm sorry I arrived late. I'd've enjoyed seeing—" Jena Rosetti fell silent when I made a broad flourish and pulled a paper flower from thin air. Bowing slightly, I presented it to her.

"For helping me try to understand Taggart's appeal."

She accepted with a curtsy, which made her look like a little match girl accepting a token of a passing nobleman's affection.

"It's not my job to understand such things," she said. "If I've sparked some understanding, please share it. My employer would be glad to hear it."

"Your employer? Who do you work for?"

"That'd be telling," she said. "I'm a buyer for an art lover who prefers to remain anonymous. Let's leave it at that."

"Is this common?"

Jena Rosetti nodded, turning back to *Subway to the Soul.*

I didn't think she was going to answer, then she said obliquely, "I don't work for him, if that's what's bothering you."

"Him?"

"Clarke Yancey. I heard from Jason what went on. He's a real son of a bitch and makes my job impossible sometimes. My employer is an art lover who doesn't want the entire world knowing what he's got in his collection—and yes, that is fairly common. Yancey outbids me more often than not. I have limits. He doesn't."

"In many different senses, that's probably true," I said.

"There're only two other paintings that appeal to me. The pair on this back panel. I'm not sure why the best of the hanging isn't out front where everyone can see it." Jena Rosetti circled a freestanding panel and pointed out the paintings.

As with the other two, these struck a chord deep inside. I wasn't even sure how I was supposed to respond. The titles matched those of the first two. Darkness poured from Taggart's paintbrush like a black waterfall.

"These four. They're the ones I'll bid on," Jena Rosetti said. "Are you bidding?"

"No. As I said, I'm just the hired help."

A small smile danced on her thin lips, then pulled back into a broader smile. "I wouldn't mind finding out what your going rate is." With that she walked off, humming to herself. I watched her vanish around another panel. For all her lack of taste in clothing, she had an undeniable style that appealed to me.

I hurried through the other paintings, not sure what I was looking at. Emerging back in the main gallery, I heard Taggart's booming voice. It was almost enough to drive me back into the more untroubled reaches of the gallery.

"Airbrush! What the fuck do you think I use on the paintings! Airbrush! That's for goddamned *illustrators*. I'm an artist, damn your eyes!"

I thought he was going to rip off Jason's head. The art critic backed away, fear flashing across his face. This seemed to be what Taggart was trying to achieve. As soon as he saw the man was terrified of him, he stopped and took a hefty slug of whatever he had in his water tumbler. From the amber flow around the ice cubes, I doubted it was iced tea.

"Something to drink, sir?" A silent waiter had glided up beside me with a silver serving tray.

"Whatever he's not having," I said, indicating Taggart. "I don't need my karma tarnished like that."

"Very good, sir." I got some soda pop that had a curiously flat taste to it. It suited me just fine. If Taggart was going to make a jackass out of himself, I didn't need to follow his lead. I didn't even need to enjoy myself.

"What are you still here for?" The demand came as I was drifting off to see if I could find Jena Rosetti again. The small woman had disappeared. Of the guests at Gloria's opening, she was the only one who struck me as the least bit civilized.

I stopped and looked over my shoulder. I tried to stay calm. Taggart had singled me out for his next attack.

"I was just leaving," I said. "I hope you have more luck selling your work than you do yourself."

"What's that mean, shit for brains?" The man's alcohol-laden breath was enough to remove the paint from his canvases. Moving back another step did no good. He followed like a Sidewinder missile locked onto a heat source.

"Very well, I'll change what I just said. I hope you starve to death in the gutter." I faced him squarely, wondering why he kept coming after me. His eyes were narrowed to slits and the rigidity of his muscles told me he'd like nothing better than to get into a fight. I tried to estimate my chances against Taggart.

He was heavier and stronger than I was. Getting into a clench or letting him land a punch would be suicidal for me. On the other hand, he was drunk and alcohol slows the reflexes—and mine were very, very good. If I kept moving, I could ruin his face with little risk of damage to me.

About the time I thought that, I shook myself out of the fantasy. There wasn't any reason to fight this loud-mouthed blowhard. He wanted to fight; I didn't.

"Go away," I said softly. "Go sleep it off and start painting again."

He lunged. All I did was sidestep. Maybe my foot was a bit slow following the rest of my body and maybe it did stiffen at just the right instant so that Taggart fell facedown on the floor. I finished the strange-tasting soda pop and put my foot squarely on his rump as he tried to sit up. Taggart crashed back to the floor.

I turned and said to Gloria, "I'll be going now. There's no need for the guest of honor to get up and see me out."

She kept from laughing. The ripple that went through the crowd told where their sympathies were. Taggart might be the featured artist but he had roundly insulted most of the guests. From some that might be a badge of honor, a mark of distinction to be noticed by some-one with Taggart's reputed talent. But deep down I think most of them knew they'd been had.

Since I didn't see her anywhere, I decided Michelle could call me later at home. We would have to get to-gether for another rehearsal. Until then, all I wanted to do was relax.

CHAPTER 10

I took my time as I gathered my gear and put the tricks away in the small case. I heaved a deep sigh. The crowd in the gallery had shrunk by half. Gloria Gadsen might have been successful; it was hard for me to tell. My own contribution to any possible financial coup was limited, I knew, with Clarke Yancey and even the guest of honor being so overtly antagonistic. Hefting the bag, I made my way out.

I paused when I heard a commotion in another of the small storerooms. I checked the crowd to see who might be in the room making such a noise. Gloria stood near the front door talking earnestly with Jason. Taggart sat in a corner and glowered at everyone. He appeared to be nursing a bruised chin from where he had hit the floor after I tripped him. Of Clarke Yancey and his pet lawyer I saw no trace. They could rot in hell for all I cared.

But the noise from the other storeroom grew louder, more insistent. I thought I heard a muffled cry but wasn't sure. Marie came bustling over to see what the trouble was. She shot me one of those cold looks of hers, as if I was to blame for whatever was going on. She pushed past without a word and tried the door. It was locked.

She started fumbling at a key ring, then swore under her breath. The noise inside grew in volume.

"I can open it, if you'd like," I said.

"The key is on my other ring." Marie frowned even more when the level of the noise rose. A few others in the gallery were beginning to notice. Marie was obviously torn between fetching her other keys or letting me try to open the door.

She made a small movement with her head that I took to mean she wanted me to try the door. It was a simple snap lock. I had several small notched pieces of spring steel with me that work well for picking locks. I can usually get out of a set of regulation handcuffs in about a minute using them. Slipping one of the slender steel strips between the doorjamb and the spring lock, I pushed and turned the knob. This door took less than three seconds to get open. Marie quickly worked in front of me and threw open the door.

"Shit," Marie muttered when she saw what was going on in the storage room.

I looked over her shoulder. My response was more physical and definitely more immediate than just standing and gawking. I pushed past her and shot into the room. I grabbed Yancey by the shoulder, shoved just enough to get him off balance, then swung as hard as I could. The movies make you think it's possible to hit someone in the chin and not suffer any injuries yourself; this is a damned good way to break every bone in your hand. I aimed squarely for his exposed throat. The force of the blow should have destroyed his Adam's apple. As luck would have it, he caught his foot on a discarded two-by-four and fell backward. The blow made him gag but didn't crush his windpipe.

Michelle Ferris clutched at her clothes and huddled down beside a large opened picture crate. She was sobbing silently. It didn't take any leap of imagination to guess what had happened to her or who was the guilty party.

Before I could follow up and finish Yancey once and for all, strong hands from behind pinned my arms to my sides. Twisting, I got free and spun to see Roy Pickering behind me. He saw the anger on my face and backed off.

"Don't," he said, his voice shrill. "I'll sue you if you so much as touch me. And Clarke'll probably sue for assault and battery—and we'll go for criminal charges against you, too. You'll spend the rest of your life behind bars, you—''

"What's happening?" Gloria Gadsen demanded. She closed the door and noticed the light was out. Grumbling, she found the switch and turned it on. Michelle was still sobbing. Clarke Yancey gobbled like a turkey and Marie just stood and stared, not saying a word. Only Roy Pickering seemed to have regained any poise.

His voice lowered, but he kept talking about lawsuits and criminal charges.

"How does attempted rape sound?" I cut in. I pointed at Michelle, "She doesn't look very consenting, does she, Pickering?"

"What do you expect?" he shot back. "She was provocatively dressed. She was asking for attention. No one can hold Mr. Yancey responsible if he gave it to her."

"When did you get your law degree? The Middle Ages? That argument went out with guys named Bubba running for governor of Texas. Gloria, call the police."

"Wait, Peter," she said. She was kneeling beside Michelle. The dark-haired woman was more in control but tears still ran down her cheeks and she shivered. "There's no need. We can work this out, just between us."

"The hell you say. He's an animal." I glowered at Yancey. "Mad dogs ought to be put down to keep them from hurting anyone else."

Roy Pickering interposed himself and helped Yancey to his feet. I was pleased to see that the so-called industrialist still wasn't able to suck in a good breath. I hadn't done any permanent harm, but the blow had taken any wind he had.

"Very well, Ms. Gadsen, let's discuss the matter in private. Without this barbarian."

"Gloria, don't let him weasel out."

"Peter," she said sharply, "you don't understand.

Stay here with Marie and Michelle. I'll be back in a few minutes.''

I helped Michelle to a box where she sat and finally stopped crying. She looked at me, her blue eyes wide. She finally said, ''Don't meddle, Peter. I don't want the police. I don't want any trouble.''

''He was the one causing the trouble,'' I said. ''You're not going to let him get away with it, are you? He was trying to rape you!''

''It . . . it's all right. I just don't want any trouble.'' She swallowed hard and finally said, ''I could never testify against him. Pickering knows about my background.''

I said nothing. Any halfway decent lawyer would rip Michelle apart on the stand. Her recent occupational background was suspect. Even more damning was her psychiatric history. The smarmy questions she would have to answer would destroy her. This was another legal collision of freedom and equality. To make Yancey pay for his attempted rape, Michelle would have to submit herself to an ordeal she'd find even worse than physical abuse. The entire world would end up thinking she was a shameless slut and a mental case.

As drunk as Clarke Yancey was, he might even get off on a plea of diminished capacity. If murder can be excused because you've been eating junk food, it should be easy to evade a rape charge if you've been drinking alcohol.

''He'll only do it again, probably to someone else.''

Marie snorted in contempt. ''From all I hear, Yancey never stops. This is his idea of a romantic good time.''

''So? Will you testify?''

''To what?'' Marie said. ''I opened the door, you ran in and hit him. I really didn't see anything.''

''You saw Michelle. You saw what he tried to do to her.'' I shut up then. If Marie wasn't willing to cooperate, a lawyer like Pickering would turn her into a defense witness when she got on the stand. That was worse than not testifying at all.

I tried to put my arm around Michelle to let her know everything was going to be all right, but she jerked away reflexively. I said nothing. I understood the reaction. In a few minutes, Gloria Gadsen returned. She looked grim but curiously satisfied. She sat down beside Michelle and comforted her.

"It's all right, dear. He's gone."

"And?" I asked. "Yancey is gone and?"

"He made some small amends. He purchased a half dozen of Taggart's paintings. I'll chose from whatever isn't sold and send those over to his office tomorrow."

"So he bought his way out. And you're letting him do it." I was struck with the unfairness of it. I know there's no such thing as fair in the world, but this rankled. Just because Yancey had money was no reason to allow him to get by with attempted rape.

I cooled off a little and realized that he *had* probably gotten by with murder—literally—during his years in business. The constant harassment by the police bringing him up on RICO charges wasn't some vagrant whim on their parts. Clarke Yancey was connected with organized crime, but money insulated him from punishment.

For the moment.

"Marie, will you take her home? I can look after the gallery."

"If she's up to it, I'll see her home," I said. I was still feeling a smoldering resentment toward both Marie and Gloria over their reactions. One didn't want to get involved and the other had turned it to her financial gain. No one was interested in Michelle Ferris.

I stopped and tried to figure out my own interest. She would make a good assistant one day. She was lovely, but I had no sexual interest in her. One person ought to help another, if possible. I might have had some small self-interest in her, not wanting to hunt for another stage assistant again this soon, but this was secondary to my outrage.

"That's all right. I . . . I don't mind if Peter sees me home."

"Very well," Gloria said somewhat coldly. She seemed angry at me for meddling. I kept my question to myself. What would she have been able to get from Yancey if she had allowed him to rape Michelle?

I reached out again to help Michelle and again she flinched away. I opened the door for her and then followed quickly, not bothering to wait for Gloria and Marie. I hefted my case and strode quickly through the gallery. The few remaining guests looked at us strangely. Jason was scribbling notes on a large yellow legal pad and Taggart hadn't moved from his chair in the corner.

I did a double take as I passed him. He growled deep in his throat like a dog on a chain straining to savage the mailman. Something about the way the light from a track mounted on the ceiling struck him made me think I'd seen him somewhere before. The cheekbones, the flame-red hair, the shape of the eyes, something about the color of the eyes—I tried to place him but couldn't. To the best of my knowledge, I'd never seen him before Gloria had mentioned the showing. I'd certainly have remembered anyone that belligerent and bellicose if I had met him before. Just shaking hands was risking getting bitten.

It just wasn't my day for making friends.

I preceded Michelle up the steps and out into Maiden Lane. I had parked over in the Union Square lot again. We walked west to it without saying a word. She was locked within herself, trying to come to grips with her own fears and thoughts. My own were well sorted, but there wasn't much I could do about them.

I opened the door for her. Michelle slid in, her arms still wrapped tightly around her body. The day wasn't that cold. She shivered visibly. I didn't bother offering her my coat. Michelle wanted silence, not politeness.

Driving up the ramp and onto Post, I wheeled around and started off.

"Where to?" I asked. "I don't know where you live."

"What? Oh, I've got an apartment in the Richmond district. Just a dinky little thing. It's all I can afford.'

"Getting your own apartment in San Francisco can cost an arm and a leg," I said, thinking about what I pay for my twentieth-story aerie. Even though I earn more than enough to pay for it, I'd still scrimp and save to be able to get a place with a good view—and high up. There's something about being able to look down on the city that relaxes me. Heaven alone knows I hadn't been able to do much of that recently, but when I do, the sight of the city in the day and the twinkling lights at night lets me believe all is well and things can work out all right.

I worked through the traffic and crossed Oak, intending to go to Masonic and then across toward the ocean. I noticed a sleek black car behind me. At first I thought nothing about it, but when it ran a stop light to maintain its position, I began to wonder.

A quick turn and then another convinced me we were being followed.

"What's wrong?" Michelle asked, noticing the sudden changes in direction.

"Street repair," I lied. "I'm making a detour. We'll get you home in a few minutes."

I drove with one eye in the mirror and the other on the traffic. Michelle gave terse directions. Within fifteen minutes I pulled up in front of a nondescript apartment building.

"This is it," she said. "You don't need to see me up."

"I will, if you want," I said.

"You're sweet, Peter, but that's okay. I just want to be alone." Her tone said she wasn't likely to do anything stupid such as try to commit suicide. I tried to catch her eye and verify my pop-psych analysis.

She reached out and put her hand on mine, pinning it to the steering wheel.

"I really will be all right. If you'd like, I'll call you later."

"I'd like," I said. "It's damned hard replacing an assistant on short notice." The little joke fell on deaf ears. If anything, it hardened her even more. Considering that her aunt had traded an assault rap for a few dollars, I should have realized this was in bad taste. "I'm sorry," I said quickly. "That was supposed to cheer you up. It's no lie, though, that I *do* need you."

She smiled weakly. "Thank you, Peter." Michelle Ferris slid from the Bimmer and rushed to the door of her apartment building. She got out her key and vanished inside without even a glance back.

I settled back in the soft leather seat and adjusted the rearview mirror. The black car was parked a block back. The tinted windshield prevented me from getting a look at the driver or any passengers.

Gunning the engine, I pulled out and decided to find out who was in the car.

CHAPTER 11

I drove around the block, expecting to come up behind the black car and see Clarke Yancey and his lawyer crawling out to follow Michelle into her apartment. To my surprise, when I rounded the block and came up from what I thought was behind, the car was gone.

Even more interesting, a quick glance into my rear view mirror showed me that the car was still following me.

Whoever was in the car wanted me, not Michelle Ferris.

I stepped on the gas and shot off. The BMW was a quick car, with plenty of power for the weight. I dashed around and screeched here and there trying to lose them. I found it was harder than I'd thought. I settled into driving steadily along the Pacific, going past the Cliff House and heading south on the Great Highway. I had no particular destination in mind, but that didn't matter. I needed the time to think of something to do. Finding out who trailed me took on increased importance.

Other thoughts crossed my mind. Yancey wanted revenge on me. He knew enough underworld types to make a simple phone call and have a hit man sent for me. This didn't seem too plausible to me as I drove, though. There had been plenty of chances for someone simply to come even with my car, pull out a gun, and start firing wildly. In this day and age, random drive-by shootings were so commonplace they hardly made the news.

I tried to lose the other car with a quick swing through

Golden Gate Park. When I got to the Arboretum and whipped past the Japanese Tea Garden, I knew there wasn't going to be a chance in hell of my getting away from them. If I wanted to find who was so diligent about wasting their gasoline pursuing me, I would have to change my tactics.

I pulled up in the parking lot in front of the De Young Museum, not caring in the least that they had a new exhibit of Medieval armor on display. I jumped out of the car and saw that my ploy had worked. It was a one-way street. Unless the black car shifted into reverse and tried to escape, it had to come by me. This would give me a chance to see who drove it—and a few seconds to pray the window wouldn't roll down and a submachine snout point at me.

To my surprise the car pulled into the parking place beside the BMW. I let out a lungful of air I had hardly known I was holding. I tried to tell myself to relax more. Breathing was the key. If I kept tensing up, dealing effectively with whatever came up would be impossible.

The car door opened and again I was surprised. Jena Rosetti stepped out, her mousy brown hair blowing in the sudden gust of wind whipping through the park.

"Hello, Mr. Thorne," she called. She slammed the door and walked over, as if we had just happened to bump into one another.

I wasn't up to witty repartee. I simply stood and stared. Too much had happened today and I wasn't at my best.

As that thought crossed my mind, I realized too much had happened in the past three days. I needed a vacation, but I wasn't likely to get one any time soon.

"Can we talk?"

"Of course, Ms. Rosetti," I said.

"Call me Jena," she said. I told her to call me Peter and we were on a more informal footing. "Do you mind if we walk?" she asked. "I've always been the nervous type. I think better when I can pace."

"The Arboretum is only a block away. It might be a little cold," I said, seeing that she wore only a thin fabric coat.

"Doesn't bother me," she said. "If anything, I prefer it that way."

We walked in silence until we got to the massive garden. We chose a path by mutual silent consent and started walking. Jena seemed to be enjoying the plants. I was thinking hard, trying to decide what was going on. I finally broke the silence.

"So?" I asked. "Why were you following me?"

She rubbed her hands together and then put them under her armpits for warmth. "That's not an easy question," she said obliquely. "I asked Gloria Gadsen about you after we'd met at the gallery."

I wasn't too favorably inclined toward Gloria at the moment. "And what did you ask her?"

"I knew you were a magician. You said that much. But I had heard your name in some other context."

"I've exposed some fake mediums," I said. "That's not too widely mentioned, though."

"Psychometry," she said. "That was what I'd heard. I asked Gloria and she said you had a talent, but she wouldn't come right out and say what it was. It *is* psychometry, isn't it?"

I turned cautious. I don't make a public display of my talent, except sometimes in the part of my act where I do the mentalist routine. Even that is usually pure stage magic, legerdemain that anyone can do with the right code words and a good assistant.

"You must be thinking of my stage act. It's just that, an act."

"No, that's not what I've heard. I hang around the cop shop a lot. I've heard the police talking about you."

"Not in any complimentary terms, I'm sure."

"They don't like outsiders. Anyone who isn't a cop is a civilian to them and therefore suspect."

She had the attitude down pretty well.

"What have you heard?"

"You can touch objects and get a picture from them. You can even tell something about the person who owns the object. It's just like the stage act, except it's for real. You've helped one of the detectives on a couple of cases. The rumbling was that you were responsible for breaking the Santorini murder a few months back."

I shuddered at the memory of that death. She had been stabbed repeatedly with a crystal blade. The blade had recorded her death throes and it screamed when I touched it. I couldn't shake the memory. And when I tried to push it aside, other, newer ones came to the surface of my mind.

The hideous death of the two bodies Worthington had pulled from the Bay. And the vibrations off the penknife and tie clip someone had passed me from the audience—those still bothered me greatly. This was a price to pay and one I didn't much like.

"There are always stories," I said. "Rumors have a way of feeding on themselves."

"But not this time. You *did* solve the murder. There was a new rumble that you and Willie Worthington are working together on another murder case."

"I don't want to talk about it." Just remembering the case brought new shivers up and down my spine. The anklet. I couldn't help remembering the plaintive message locked in it.

Don't! The pain! Stop it, stop hurting me!

"Are you all right, Peter? You look pale."

"Feeling a bit under the weather," I said. There didn't seem to be any good reason to go into the real reason I was suddenly dizzy and my head felt like someone was playing golf with it. If only Jena Rosetti hadn't brought up the psychometry. The mention of my talent triggered the memories. I sneezed and wiped my nose and tried to get the smell out of my nostrils. The strange sense-confusing psychometry had made me smell raw onions this time.

"You might have a cold," she said solicitously.

"You've gone to a lot of trouble to track me down. Other than my charming self, what is it?"

"You don't have a very high opinion of yourself, do you?" She turned and looked squarely at me, her brown eyes wide. "That's a shame. You've got a lot on the ball. And even though we've only talked a few minutes, I think I could like you."

"I'm sorry if I didn't think you wanted anything more than to make use of my psychometry talent." I saw that I'd hit the heart of the matter by the wash of guilt across Jena's face.

"I confess. I'm intrigued by you. I'm also getting close to desperation and need your help."

"Psychometry isn't something I can turn on and off like a faucet," I said. "I need to concentrate, and it takes a great deal of my energy. There are other side effects I don't even want to mention."

"My reputation's at stake," Jena said. "I told you I'm a buyer for anonymous art collectors. I also appraise and do some insurance work, but that's not what's got my tail in a wringer."

It didn't take much to guess where this was leading. "You've bought a painting that you think is a fake."

"You *are* good," she said in admiration. "But then I don't suppose it was that hard a guess, was it?"

"Not really." We walked along for several yards before I came to my conclusion. "I'll do it, if you can assure me of a few things."

"Anything, Peter. I really appreciate this. I do!"

"This has to be considered nothing but a not-too-good check on authenticity. I'm no art authority. Just looking at it I won't be able to tell. I'm not even sure I'll have any success as a psychometrician."

"Please try. It's very important." There was no denying her earnestness. There was almost a panic to her tone, too. And I found myself liking her more and more. There was a lack of pretense in Jena Rosetti that appealed to me.

"You've got to assure me there's no crime involved."

"Oops," she said. "Can't. If this is a forgery, then fraud has been committed. Art forgery isn't as top-drawer stuff as drug dealing these days, but the profits are immense."

"That's all right. What I meant was, no one's died because of this."

The question rocked her back. Her mouth opened, then closed. She finally got her thoughts straight. "I don't know of anyone who's died. The last person I know who kicked the bucket was my uncle. He smoked himself to death. Emphysema. But that was over two years ago."

"Violent death is what I meant. No murders?"

"None."

"I'll give it a try. Remember, I don't know what I can scope out on this. You might be better off taking the painting to a lab and having a chemical workup done on it."

"My usual tech is off on vacation for two weeks. My . . . employer is getting really antsy over this. There are other ways to determine if the painting is legit, but I don't have time for those tests."

"NMR?"

"Are you *sure* you're not an art expert? Nuclear magnetic resonance is one way. They did some of that on the Shroud of Turin—and I won a bet with a friend. Told her the shroud only dated back to the early Middle Ages."

"I'm no expert," I assured her. "Where is the painting?"

"At my place, over in Sausalito. We can be there in a half hour. Just catch Park Presidio down to One-oh-one and across the Golden Gate."

"Let's go," I said.

She paused for a moment and then said, a twinkle in her eye, "There might even be dinner in this for you. The hors d'oeuvres Gloria served were awful."

"How can I refuse?"

We returned to the parking lot, now almost empty. The cold, damp air was making me sneeze and cough. I hoped this wasn't the start of a full-blown cold. It's hell trying to perform with a stopped up nose. My voice always sounds tinny and taking too many antihistamines causes my reflexes to slow just enough for me to botch up the more complicated tricks.

Maybe what I needed was for Jena to cook me a good dinner. I was beginning to hope she could cure some of what ailed me. She drove off. I followed her taillights through the park north to 101 and then across the bridge. We went through the tunnel with the rainbow painted over it and then immediately began winding down toward the harbor. I began to suspect that she lived on a small houseboat. When she pulled up to the pier and pointed out a visitors' parking area, I knew I was right. I was beginning to think I could foresee the future as well as psychometrize.

"I do appreciate this, Peter. There'll be a generous fee, too. I'll split my commission with you on it."

"We'll see," I said. "What's the problem other than it being a fraud?"

"I don't know if it is," she said. "Accusing the man who sold it to me—to my employer—is a bit risky. I thought it was legitimate but the more I studied it the less sure I became. I have a chance of returning it and getting back the money I paid if I act fast."

"Otherwise, you might be giving a fake to your employer," I said.

"If I do that and he finds out, it'd be curtains for me."

"Everyone makes a mistake," I pointed out.

Jena Rosetti shook her head and shuddered with dread. "Not when you're dealing with men like him. I don't much like him, but he's got one hell of a budget for artwork." The nearness to panic I had felt before returned. It didn't suit her.

"Let's take a look at the painting," I said. She

jumped lithely onto a small houseboat. I followed her into the main cabin. I wasn't quite sure what I expected but this wasn't it. The cabin was almost bare of artwork.

Jena saw the surprise on my face. She shrugged and said, "The kind of work I like is very expensive. I'd rather buy just one or two pieces than clutter the place with inferior work. For instance, take a look at this."

She opened a low cabinet and took out a small bronze. It was delicately formed and involved my eye immediately. I traced the sleek lines with my eyes and started to touch it. I caught myself before I did.

"That's all right," she said. "Statuary is meant to be touched. Go on." She held it out for me. It proved far heavier than I'd anticipated.

I sat down on a chair and placed the figurine on the table in front of me. There was a warmth emanating from the statue. I closed my eyes and let my senses float and soar, dip and slid through onto another plane. I saw the heat from the piece, an inner fire infused into it by its creator. I heard the light glancing off it and I tasted the sleekness as I drew my fingers along the sweeping lines.

The sensory jumble was pleasant, almost restful and warm and pale green and gardenia-scented with a cinnamon flavor. I had forgotten psychometry could be like this. Worthington always involved me in the nasty crimes, and I seldom explored the astral realms where I now paused. Psychometry was a gift—or it could be. I had come to think of it as more of a curse.

"It's cleansing," I said. "There's an energy to it that both soothes and excites."

"Do you know who sculpted it?"

"I don't have any idea," I said. Even as I spoke flashes came into my mind. I saw odors and heard a forge working. "It's old. But not too old. Maybe a hundred years."

"It's a working model from Rodin's *The Burghers of Calais* and dates back to 1885."

"He had passion."

"And you do have a great talent, Peter." Jena was excited now. She went to a shallow storage locker and pulled out a two-by-three-foot painting. The cracks in the surface showed where varnish had aged and chipped off. A part of the painting itself was missing, bare canvas poking through.

"This is it? It looks even older than the bronze."

"I thought so, too, at first. Now I have doubts. I won't go into all the reasons I'm worried about this, but the chipped area is part of it. The old masters often overpainted a half dozen times. There's no evidence there's anything under the top layer."

"They reused their canvases?"

"Times were hard and even the wealthiest patrons didn't always like what their resident artists did for them. So it was back to the drawing boards, usually over the rejected work."

I shook my head. I was learning a great deal I didn't know about painting. The Japanese woodcuts I fancied were quite simple in comparison, even though it often took a half dozen skilled workmen besides the artist to produce a print.

Placing the painting in front of me on the table, Jena Rosetti stepped back as if expecting me to burst into flame and take her with me. I closed my eyes and settled my mind once more. The trance came easily this time. I remembered the gentle passion locked in the Rodin bronze and yearned for more.

I placed my hands on the surface. Jena gasped but said nothing. My eyes remained closed as I tried to absorb all the impressions I could from the work. At first there was nothing. I was alone on the astral plane, walking along with clouds and vapors and mist rising all about me. A few odd smells caught my attention. I turned and looked directly at the painting. It shimmered as if it had been caught in a heat mirage.

Then the vision was gone and I was again alone. I heaved a deep sigh and leaned back. Jena rushed forward with a cloth to patch up any damage my skin oils might have done to the painting.

"Don't bother," I said. "It's supposed to be old, right? It can't date back more than a few months. I caught the impression of heat, but I wasn't sure."

"A drying oven?"

I shrugged. I couldn't say. The impressions hadn't been that intense. "Whoever did this work had no emotional stake in it. I'm not able to psychometrize nonmetallic objects as well as I can metallic ones, but there are subtle vibrations. There's very little to this painting."

Jena just stood and stared. I tried to put my impressions into better order to explain to her.

"Remember the paintings of Taggart's you pointed out to me. Those had a vitality to them this lacks. I didn't even have to touch them to sense it. Even the ones that Taggart did that aren't so somber and menacing had a small hint of animation to them. If I could touch those paintings, I'm sure it would give me a spark like the Rodin."

"It's a fake," she said in a dull voice, staring at the painting on the table. "Damnation. This is going to be hell."

"You said you could take it back to the dealer and—" I saw that she hadn't been telling me the truth on this score. She had already purchased the painting and could never return it. I had to ask why this was impossible.

"There's a gray market for paintings," she explained. "No questions asked, cash money only, and who knows where the seller is now."

"Stolen paintings?"

Jena started crying. "I only do what he tells me. He wanted it so badly, but he'll kill me when he finds out I spent a quarter million on a fake."

"Don't tell him. Let him think it's the real thing." This was patent dishonesty but it was all I could think of to calm Jena Rosetti.

"It's not that easy. This is going on display when he

gets it. Oh, not to the public but a dozen critics will see it in a private hanging. Someone will blow the whistle on me. Oh, God, I'm ruined!''

"It doesn't seem you're all that guilty. He almost forced you to buy.''

"You don't understand. He gets what he wants, but it had better be value for the money spent. He's one hell of a—never mind, Peter. Thank you for coming. I was afraid you'd come to the same conclusion I had.''

"I might be wrong.''

Jena Rosetti shook her head, tears still flowing. "I didn't want to admit it to myself. There's no denying it now.''

"You promised me dinner. Let me buy. I know a good restaurant down by the wharf. They . . .'' My voice trailed off when I saw she wasn't interested.

"I am sorry, Peter. I promised you. Maybe later, after this has blown over.'' She forced a smile to her lips. "I might even make you buy. I doubt I'll be getting any more work after this.'' She sucked in her breath and then said, "I almost forgot. I promised you half of my commission on this.''

She started for a cabinet. I stopped her.

"That's all right. Keep the money. Giving back your commission might cool off your hotheaded patron of the arts.''

"Yeah, maybe. Thanks, Peter, you're one in a million.''

I decided it was time to take my leave. It hadn't been a remarkably good day. And it wasn't going to get any better.

CHAPTER 12

The evening had taken more turns than I would have thought when I got up this morning. The performance at Gloria Gadsen's gallery had turned into a fiasco. It had been stupid of me to provoke Clarke Yancey the way I had, yet looking back there didn't seem to be any way to have avoided the outcome. He was an asshole and that was all there was to it. He would have assaulted Michelle no matter what I had or hadn't done earlier.

I heaved a deep sigh and shook my head as I thought about the artist Gloria had tried to honor with the showing. Taggart was a drunkard and probably dangerous when intoxicated. Still, there was a disturbing quality to his work that was the trademark of good art. Jason the art critic had commented on it and so had Jena Rosetti.

She was probably the biggest disappointment of the day. I found myself attracted to her. There was a quickness of wit and intelligence that danced and gambolled. I was sorry I hadn't been able to tell her everything would be fine with the painting she had purchased for her employer. Still, I found it hard to believe whomever she worked for would be as intolerant as Jena made out. The art world seemed to be full of thieves—and damned good ones. Faking a masterpiece was something a handful of modern artists did extremely well. With technology on their side to artificially age and duplicate pigments lost for centuries, it must be an impossible task to be one hundred percent sure of authenticity on every painting.

I remembered reading about a Mondrian that had been forged. The dealer and the forger had been caught because they hadn't known Mondrian used masking tape, at the time a brand new convenience, in laying out his lines. Small leakage under the tape prevented razor-sharp edges from being crafted. Their forgery was too good, if that was possible.

I decided I would call Jena when I got to my apartment, just to be sure she was all right. She had been trying to hide her dread. The more I thought about it, the more imperative it became to call her. She wasn't just apprehensive, she was scared to death. There wasn't much I could do to help her other than lend moral support, but I found that I wanted to do whatever I could. Talking with her employer was probably out of the question. Anyone demanding such secrecy had no desire to allow a stage magician in to talk about art. If Jena told me who she worked for, that might make her position even worse.

I have to park my car about ten blocks down the hill from my apartment. It turns out to be cheaper by several hundred dollars a month and the hike isn't usually too onerous. Tonight I was bone tired and the steep hill seemed like Mt. Everest. By the time I reached the lobby, I was winded and ready to fall asleep.

The ride to the twentieth floor went quickly; there wasn't anyone else stirring at two in the morning. Most people had to be at work in a few hours and if their weekends had been the least bit exciting, they were safely asleep in their beds.

I hesitated outside the door to my apartment. Most people might be securely asleep, but someone had been up and about. And they'd been in my apartment.

The door stood slightly ajar. I'm obsessive about locks and always lock up when I leave, whether it's a car or my apartment. Even if I only leave for a few minutes, I always lock up. Thinking back, I tried to remember if this had been the one time I had grown careless. Had I been in a rush to get to Gloria's for the performance?

I hadn't.

Running my fingers up and down the side of the door revealed jagged splinters. Someone had used a crowbar to rip the dead bolt expertly from the doorjamb. Shifting position, I saw where the wreckage lay inside the room. A single powerful jerk had torn it free. Carefully touching the doorknob, I noticed that it spun freely. Vise grips had been fastened to the knob and then tightened and spun hard. A single revolution had snapped the internal locking mechanism.

It had taken someone all of twenty seconds to break into my apartment. The cautions about entering a burgled house came back. The robbers might still be inside. Surprise them and you might end up on the business end of a pistol or knife. If there were several of them, they could pile on and beat you to death. Why add assault and possible murder to the list of charges against them when you could stop the crime spree by simply not going in?

I went in anyway. The tiredness had turned itself into cold fury. I had been pushed around, Michelle had almost been raped, Jena Rosetti was in trouble with her boss, and there was damned little I had done all day long to vent my frustration. As reckless as it was, I hoped the burglar *was* still inside. I'd rip him limb from limb.

It was probably just as well I didn't get my chance to duke it out with a would-be robber. My apartment was empty—and it had been thoroughly trashed. Furniture had been overturned, my precious magic posters had been ripped from the walls and left in piles of confetti, drawers had been opened and emptied on the floor.

Worst of all was the desecration done to the far wall. A single lamp had been placed on the floor, the shade adjusted so that it shone the light directly onto the inverted pentagram drawn crudely on the wall. I walked over and sniffed.

The familiar coppery scent of blood grew stronger the closer I got to the wall. I saw where tiny streaks had run down the plaster as the pentagram had been hastily applied. The heat from the lamp had dried the blood quickly. There wasn't any way to tell how long ago the vandals had trashed my place. I made a quick tour through the rest of the apartment and found my clothing slashed and thrown onto the floor. The sink had been plugged with some black, sticky substance; it didn't take a genius to figure out the gunk had hardened in the pipes and would require a plumber to replace everything.

My landlord wasn't going to be happy with me after tonight. I called the police.

The only spot they had left untouched was the balcony. I went out and sat in the chair, oblivious of the cold, wet wind blowing off the Bay. A hint of fog had drifted in, obscuring Sausalito and Jena Rosetti's houseboat. From the way the shoreline curled back at Tiburon I doubted I could even see her houseboat using binoculars, but it was a decent enough fantasy to spend the time while I waited for the cops. It took them forty-five minutes to show up. Either it was a busy night or they had to finish their coffee and doughnuts before attending to such a minor crime.

I ought to have told them Colombian drug lords had invaded the city. That would have gotten half the city police force out, not to mention the DEA and the FBI.

They came in with guns drawn. I raised my hands and introduced myself. "The vandals are long gone. I'm the one who called you."

The policeman didn't lower his weapon. He kept it trained directly at me. I wondered if he would shoot when I was unable to hold back the sneeze building up. Trying not to sneeze and to keep my hands up made me shake all over.

"You on drugs? That why you did this?"

"If you need character references, call Detective Sergeant Willie Worthington."

"Who's that?" the cop asked suspiciously.

"He's a friend of mine in homicide."

"Someone get wasted?" came the question from the other room. The cop's partner came out, hand on her service revolver. She didn't worry me. The one who had the drop on me did. He had one of the new Glock automatics. He could rip me apart with eighteen slugs before he bothered to reload and keep firing.

"No one's been killed that I know of," I said. "I was vandalized and your partner thinks I did all this myself."

"We can't take any chances," she said. She pushed back a strand of dishwater blond hair and said, "Let's see some ID."

Getting cute and telling her to fish it out of my rear pocket would have gotten me blown away. I indicated where it was and reached very slowly, keeping my hands in view and showing that it really was a wallet being pulled from my pocket. I opened it to my driver's license and held it out.

She advanced, careful not to get in the line of fire. I was beginning to get angry. *I* was the aggrieved party, not the culprit. They were treating me as if I had just made the FBI's 10 Most Wanted List.

"Peter Thorne," she said. "Of this address."

"Picture match?" asked her partner, almost disappointed that he wasn't going to get an easy kill tonight. I'd have to talk to Worthington about this. Being a police officer isn't an easy job and routine calls are usually where most cops get killed, but this procedure wasn't winning the hearts and minds of the civilians.

"Yeah, it's a match," she said. She still backed away to let her partner waste me if it was necessary. "What happened?"

"I came home and found my place like this." A wide flourish showed the wreckage. "I've looked around and can't find anything missing. But whoever did it was incredibly thorough in trashing everything. Clothes, belongings, everything.''

The male cop was standing in front of the bloody pentagram and scribbling away in his notebook. He flipped the spiral book shut and turned after a few seconds.

''That's a wrap on this one, Linda. There's no need to get too deep in it. Satanists.''

''What?'' This was incredible. ''You take one look at *that* and say it was done by Satanists?''

''Who else? Damned kids get coked up and listen to heavy metal music, then they go and do dumb things like this. We'll ask around to see if anyone heard the kids when they came in. There's not much chance we'll ever catch them.''

''Or try to catch them,'' I said. ''Aren't you going to call forensics and have them look for fingerprints? Clues?''

''We could. They might be a day or two getting out, though. You could live in a hotel till then. We'd have to put the entire place under a cordon.'' The cop smiled, amused at me wanting justice done now.

''Days? Why not now?''

''They've got things to do,'' the woman said.

''And your watch commander doesn't like you annoying them, keeping them from real crimes, is that it?''

''You said it, I didn't.'' She made another quick circuit through the place and returned. ''Never saw trashers use tar in a sink before. They're getting a little more imaginative.''

''How happy I am for them,'' I said sarcastically. ''Could that possibly mean this wasn't done by teenagers?''

''Who you made mad recently, Mr. Thorne?'' she asked. ''Sometimes you cut them off in traffic and they flip you off and then you come home to this. Other times, you bump into them on the street or in a park and this happens. Weird kids we have these days.''

They hadn't convinced me that teenagers, whether on cocaine or listening to Ozzie Osborne or even into Satanism, had done this.

"Why just me?"

"Maybe you were the only one out tonight," the other cop said. "They ring doorbells and if someone answers or tells them to beat it, they move on. You didn't answer and—" He made a sweeping gesture showing the penalty for being away from home.

"This is a security building," I said. "They couldn't get in without a key."

"Or being buzzed in by a resident," the female cop finished. "That's just about as easy as anything in the world. How do you think we got in?"

I considered it. They hadn't rung my apartment. "The manager?"

"I just started pushing buttons until someone let us in to stop us from disturbing their sleep. We didn't want to ring here if the robbers—the vandals—were still inside."

I saw they weren't going to do any real investigating. I started going through the piles of debris, trying to find something I'd overlooked. When I came to my *ukiyo-e* I stopped. Several Hokusai prints from the *Mangwa* collection were untouched, as were the Hiroshiges. They had been dumped onto the floor but they weren't ripped apart like my theater posters. This got me to thinking. I must have missed something else.

"We're going to file our report. Here's the report number of your insurance, and if you come across anything you think we might be able to use to find the perpetrators, call this number." He dropped a card on a table by the door and left. I heard the two of them chattering like magpies all the way to the elevator.

Sitting down, I began my relaxation meditations. This cleared my thinking and took some of the edge off my nerves. Mentally sorting through the things I should and shouldn't do helped push away the implications of my apartment's trashing.

Calling Jena Rosetti was out of the question now. It was past three in the morning. I had to call Michelle Ferris, too, but that could wait until much later. Other points of my schedule came and went. Most were insignificant but it helped me to think about them for a few seconds before moving on. It returned my life to a more ordered existence and banished the chaos that had entered.

When I was more composed I went and figured out how to close the door and prop it shut. Then I started my systematic cleanup. When I had come home, my eyes were gauzy with sleep. That had been erased entirely. I'd have to catnap later. Now I had to go through the mess and get some semblance of order restored.

As I worked, small details kept returning to annoy me. The pentagram in blood reeked so badly I left the balcony door open to air the place out. The cold wind helped keep my mental edge and gave the apartment the cleansing freshness it needed. And I kept coming back to the *ukiyo-e* woodcuts. They hadn't been damaged, other than incidentally when other things fell on top of them. Why not?

Other things seemed out of place. I couldn't buy the police officers' contention this had been a random crime. Coming prepared with crowbars, tar and buckets of blood seemed a bit farfetched. On impulse I opened the door and examined the hallway. There wasn't a trace of spilled blood or tar. I checked both elevators. Nothing. I even went downstairs and, on hands and knees, crawled through the lobby and carefully studied the floor of the entryway.

No blood. No tar.

Would coked up heavy metal Satanists be this neat until they got to my apartment—and only my apartment? I didn't think I would have to ask my neighbors if they had been disturbed. Someone had honed in on me and me alone. I was the target and it wasn't random.

Back in the apartment I checked the rug and found only traces of blood under the pentagram. They hadn't even splashed the blood around after they got inside.

Something else began to bother me. I walked slowly through the apartment looking for all the items I knew belonged there. Everything was there. Nothing had been taken.

Or had it? I returned to the living room and made a careful search that lasted more than an hour for the penknife and the tie clip that had come to me through my stage performance.

Both were missing.

CHAPTER 13

The telephone rang about 8:15. I grumbled as I rolled over and grabbed for it. I knocked it off the stand but caught the cord as the handset plunged to the floor. Working like a fisherman with a berserk fish on the line, I reeled in the phone.

"Hello? Is anyone there?"

"Thorne speaking. What do you want?"

"I'm sorry to disturb you, Mr. Thorne, but our meeting room was double booked. We need to rearrange the time. I know this is a last-minute inconvenience but—"

"Meeting room?" I wasn't awake yet. Getting to bed after five and then being awakened by the ringing phone wasn't what it took to put me in a good mood. I had meant to turn on the answering machine but had forgotten. Remembering what had happened last night, I wasn't even sure it was still in working condition. So much had been ruined. The vandals had not only clogged my drains with tar, they had destroyed my microwave and shorted out my refrigerator. I don't know how long it had taken them to work over my apartment, but they had done a good job of it.

"Peter Thorne?"

"Yes, dammit, who is this?" I wasn't in a good mood at all.

"Sorry, I'm Jeremy Mason. I'm secretary for the Committee to Explain the Paranormal. You were supposed to give a talk to us at noon today. We lost the room and were wondering if you could make it at ten-thirty?"

I had forgotten about the talk. Great control kept me from moaning aloud. I needed sleep, not more speaking engagements. But several friends were members of this group and I had promised them months ago I would speak to the organization of skeptics.

"This must be terribly inconvenient," he offered, when I could summon no response. "We can cancel the meeting, if you're unable to speak."

"That's all right, Mr. Mason," I said, wondering why I did things like this to myself. Heaving to a sitting position, I stretched and tried to remember what I had done with the prepared notes for the talk. If they were in my desk, they'd been turned to confetti better than anything that ever went through Oliver North's shredding machine.

"Same restaurant, just a couple hours earlier. Thanks, Mr. Thorne. We appreciate it."

"See you there." I collapsed back to the bed and stared at the ceiling, trying to make patterns out of the bumps in the plaster. Nothing came to me, a bad sign. Usually constellations form and sea waves crash and rockets soar; strange new magic tricks even suggest themselves. This morning: nothing.

Giving up, I heaved myself out of bed and went into the bathroom. I had forgotten the drains were clogged. I ran some water into a plastic bowl and washed that way. I needed a bath but it would have to wait. The suggestion about staying in a motel for a few days seemed better by the minute.

I called the manager of the apartment and told him what had happened. He grumbled and swore a bit but said he'd get the maintenance supervisor up to look over the place. There wasn't any need to arrange for a passkey. He would come in whenever he wanted.

Then I tried calling Jena Rosetti to see how she was faring. The phone rang a dozen times. I figured she must already be over at her employer's trying to explain how she had lost a quarter of a million dollars of his money. It wasn't a meeting I wanted to attend; it would be bad enough hearing about it later.

My clothing was filthy from everything I'd been through yesterday and I didn't have any usable clothing left. I finished a quick, simple breakfast and then left for the Rialto. I had several changes of clothing in my dressing room. I picked the one most in keeping with an informal situation, even though most were the swallowtails and cutaways I used in my act. By this time I was just a little late getting to the restaurant off Divisadero where the would-be debunkers held their monthly meetings.

Hurrying in, I quickly found the meeting room in the back. Almost two dozen had turned out for the early lecture.

"So glad you could make it," a short, stout man gushed. This had to be Jeremy Mason.

"Sorry to be late. Things have been hectic lately," I said, not wanting to itemize all that had gone wrong in the twenty-four hours. I still had to call Michelle Ferris and arrange for a late-afternoon rehearsal, if she still wanted to work with me. After the set-to at her aunt's gallery, she might not want even to be in the public eye any longer.

"Sit here. Is there anything we can get you? We didn't know what to order."

"Tea, please," I said. "I don't drink coffee."

The hot tea came and I sipped slowly. It was too strong, but who cared? It warmed me all the way down to my stomach and let me relax more than I had in days. Members came and went. I didn't try to remember their names, but I stood occasionally to shake hands and move among them. The meeting was called to order and I was able to start a second cup of tea. By the time Mason had finished the introductions, I was ready to tell them what I knew of fake mediums and what to look for in debunking them.

I spoke for a while about the mechanisms used by frauds, then launched into a detailed discussion of

Magyar and how I had decided on approaching him. The discussion went well with questions until that well ran dry.

"He was a fake healer," came a question from the audience. "Have you ever exposed any fortune tellers or astrologers?"

I smiled wanly. Those were my special mission in life. My wife had died because an astrologer had told her to listen only to a faith healer. The two had worked together and she had died of cancer. It might have been inoperable, but there was always a small chance with medical science rather than pure faith.

I didn't want to get into the story of Marla Wise and Damien Bishop but another came to me, one that had happened only a month earlier.

"There was one astrologer who went by the name of Lady MacDowell. I never did learn her real name. She used several of the more traditional bilking schemes as well as casting charts. Her favorite was a modification of the Gypsy pigeon drop."

I saw that they weren't familiar with this variation on the old scheme.

"She cast horoscopes telling her clients something terrible was going to happen to them, but that she could avert it—for a price. The usual spiel was a loss of money, but that was all right because she could safeguard it for them or even make it grow.

"The money was handed over, and Lady MacDowell put it into a sealed box and returned it to them. She cast new horoscopes, all of which cost additional money, and had her victims moving the box as many as three or four times a week. Each move cost them a bit more for her prognosticating powers."

I cleared my throat as I remembered Lady MacDowell. She had an accent so thick it could be cut with a knife. This lent an air of authority to everything she said. After all, she was a foreigner and knew of things mere Americans never could. Or so the prejudice usually ran.

With the memory of Lady Macdowell came other thoughts, twisting and turning and making me just a bit dizzy. I sipped more tea as I clutched the small podium and tried to keep from weaving. I hoped the audience didn't notice. Odds and ends came rushing back to me, and I couldn't force them away.

The anklet. *Nooo!* Pain and the loss of a finger, an arm, more. Slowly. More and more being cut off, inch by inch. *Stop it! Don't torture me. Why are you doing this to me?*

"She finally cast a horoscope that told them to bury the box until the next full moon, which conveniently happened in about a month's time. By then she'd be far gone." My voice sounded gravelly and distant to me. I took a deep breath to keep going with the talk. I couldn't give in to the images slashing at my brain. They were leftovers from psychometrizing the woman's anklet, nothing more.

"And the money was missing?" guessed Jeremy Mason. "She had switched it? How?"

"Easy sleight of hand," I said. "Let me see your wallet for moment, will you?" I took it but as he handed it to me, it slipped from my fingers and fell to the floor. I stooped and retrieved it.

Mason took it back, a perplexed look on his face. "I don't understand," he said. "You didn't do anything."

"Look inside." As he dug around I began holding up the fourteen dollars he had carried in folding money and started fanning through the charge cards I had filched. The laughter made Mason turn red. I handed the money and cards back.

"Don't think I am picking on Mr. Mason. It could have happened to any of you."

"These aren't my credit cards!" Mason blurted out. He looked around the table and then *he* started laughing. He passed out the cards to the people I had pickpocketed earlier as I had been introduced to them.

"There are many ways of switching the contents of a box, even when you're on your guard," I said. "Lady

MacDowell was expert at this. She intended to be in Vancouver by the time the first of her suckers dug up the box of money and found only cut paper in it.

"This wasn't the full impact of her pitch, though," I continued. "She had several customers who had put their life savings into their boxes rather than risk whatever loss she had contrived astrologically for them. Since everything they had was in the box, she had them charge major appliances, TV sets, stereos, microwaves, on their credit cards and give it all to her as payment for her horoscopes. The appliances she sold, and her customers were left penniless and stuck with a mountain of bills."

"You stopped her?"

"Yes," I said. I recalled discussing the case with Michelle. "She committed suicide rather than face the police."

I wobbled once more, remembering that she had blown herself to smithereens and had blamed me for it.

Scissors. I hate scissors. Take them away!

I closed my eyes and tried to ride out the waves of mixed up sensations assaulting me. This had come from the tie clip that had been stolen from my apartment. It had no connection with the woman who had been cut in half, but my talent isn't able to separate such thoughts. Reeling from cross-connected senses, I saw taste and heard light and felt odors.

Pain! Why are you doing scissors no please why torture some kind of joke pain, burning pain, searing, cutting pain!

"Mr. Thorne, are you all right?"

"Sorry. Just a bit woozy. I didn't get much sleep last night. What was the question?"

I talked about how easy it was to pick pockets, and to set up the proper lighting and fiber optics displays to give the illusion of spirit guides. The people were informed well enough on technical matters but lacked a feeling for the corkscrew minds most con artists have. This was what always put the honest man or woman at a disadvantage. They couldn't quite believe anyone was out to con them.

And the ones who were aware of con artists were sure everyone was out to get them. That often made them even easier marks. They overexamined and missed the simple scams. I had seen some of them go to elaborate lengths to plot a double cross when they had already been taken and didn't even realize it.

I concluded the talk and sat down to polite applause. Sweat beaded on my forehead and I finished my tea, hoping this would calm the storms raging inside my head. If anything, the caffeine caused new vortices to form and suck me into them.

Pushed and pulled, prodded and kicked by my psychometric memories, I found Lady MacDowell mixed in with the half woman Worthington had pulled from the Bay and the tie clip passed to me during my performance. The kinetic sights and sounds whipped around my head and made it almost impossible to concentrate.

I excused myself before they started their business meeting and left. There was too much I had to do—and the way my psychometric talents were acting up today, I wasn't sure I could accomplish much of anything except returning to bed and trying to quell the confusing rush.

CHAPTER 14

The last thing in the world I needed was to have Willie Worthington call me, but he did. If I were any kind of psychic, I would have known that it would be pure hell to return to my apartment. But I did. Sometimes I wonder about my common sense.

The phone was ringing as I went in. I was preoccupied with the need to call Michelle Ferris to arrange for an afternoon rehearsal, and there was a call I needed to make to Jena Rosetti to find out how she had fared. And the police hadn't done much in the way of investigating the break-in and vandalism in my apartment. I needed to check on their progress and to keep a fire built under them. And the landlord hadn't done a damned thing about replacing the lock on the door.

A world of things needed tending and Worthington called. I was less than polite.

"What do you want?" I snapped when I heard his pleasant voice.

"My, my, we got up on the wrong side of the bed this morning, didn't we?"

"My place was vandalized. I am lucky to even *have* a bed. What do you want?"

"A bit of civility will go a long way," Worthington said, his voice turning melancholy. "It hasn't been the greatest of days for me either. One of my squad finally went around the bend and ate a bullet this morning about three A.M.."

"So we're agreed on something; everyone has problems. I'm sorry to hear one of your officers killed himself. The one who killed the boy?"

Worthington snorted in contempt. ''Would you believe it? It was his partner. Go figure. I've got a squad room filled with mental basket cases and the files are piling up on my desk. We had another murder not twenty minutes ago—drug related. I'm foisting it of on the DEA boys. They seemed to want a piece of it, so to hell with 'em all. Anything to get a break in the progress of society.''

''Willie, why did you call? You could have called the department's psychiatrist if you needed to talk things out. Or call a priest and confess. They're professionals. They listen. They *want* to listen. It gives them a feeling of being needed. Me, it gives a feeling of indigestion.''

''I've been doing some digging. You want to come on down to the station? Some of the items might amuse you.''

''Nothing will amuse me,'' I said tiredly. I glanced at my watch and decided I had the time. I shouldn't really go driving all the way across town, but something in Worthington's voice told me I should. More than that, some inner feeling told me I ought to see what he had turned up.

''See you in a half hour,'' Worthington said, reading my tone properly. I was left with a dial tone in my ear. I dropped the phone into its cradle before the obnoxious beeping started to tell me the phone was off the hook. The phone company charges extra for everything, but I'd pay gladly to be able to turn off that annoying sound.

Fiddling with my low-tech answering machine, I finally got a red light to come on showing that it was getting power. Whether it worked right was beyond my guessing. The only person I really wanted to speak to was Michelle Ferris.

I corrected that. There were a couple of people I wanted to talk to. I gave Jena Rosetti a call again but there was no answer. I let the phone ring a few times and decided she must be having one heavy meeting with her employer. She might be in the city and tied up all day. I'd have to catch her later. The thought that she might need my cheering up later cheered me up somewhat now.

Hope springs eternal, after all.

That settled my one social call for the time being. I went over to business calling, dialed Michelle, and got her on the third ring. "Are you up for a rehearsal this afternoon?" I asked.

"Yes, of course, Peter. What time?"

"Let's make it three o'clock," I said, calculating how much time it would take to get back and forth to the Hall of Justice where Worthington's office was. "I've got a couple errands to run before we get together, but then we can get down to serious work. Are you sure you still want to do the show tonight?"

"Of course," she said, sounding surprised. I almost asked how she was doing.

I felt like the woman who couldn't stop taking in stray kittens.

"See you at the Rialto at three," I said, making sure she understood.

I tried to call the landlord but his line was busy. I found that I couldn't use the toilet; something other than tar had been used to stop it up. Muttering to myself I took the elevator down and banged on the landlord's door until he answered. He obviously wasn't too happy to see me.

"At least fix the lock on my door. There's not much left inside worth stealing, but there are a few things," I said.

"I been trying. You don't know how hard it is to get someone out inside a week." From the way he squinted and looked at me, he was trying to come up with an excuse to throw me out of the building. I wasn't going to give him the chance. I liked my place, I loved the view of the Bay, and I wasn't going to move.

"My lawyer's working on the insurance claims now," I said. The mere mention of getting a lawyer involved always seemed to pour oil on turbulent waters.

"Yeah, I'll get on it. There's a kid in the building

who might want to pick up a few extra bucks doing handiwork. The pipes are one fucking mess.''

"I noticed," I said dryly. I left before I got into a long conversation with him. I paid my rent on time and didn't give the neighbors any cause to complain. I didn't need lectures on being a good tenant or his sidling ways of trying to throw me out. It just wasn't the kind of day where I could put up with such nonsense.

The drive across town ended almost before it seemed to begin. My mind was drifting to things other than traffic. This was dangerous but I was parked in the Hall of Justice lot before I knew it. I made my way through the hordes of workmen replastering the immense lobby. They must have numbered more than the people who usually worked in the building. I wondered what it would take to have a couple of them go to my apartment and redo the wall with the bloody pentagram on it. The city wouldn't miss a few of them, not with this many avidly featherbedding on the city timeclock.

Wending my way through barricades and sawhorses, I found Willie Worthington's office just off the squad room. He has a small frosted glass enclosure that's not much more than a cubbyhole. He can look out over the bustle of the room without having to go out. A simple window blind blocks out what's happening in his office, if he wants to be that secretive. In all the years I've known Worthington, I've never once seen the blind pulled down. It might not even work.

Seeing the detective, I thought the same thing might be said of him. He always had his feet hiked up on his desk, usually with a soda pop and a hot dog or two in a greasy paper wrapper balanced on the edge of his desk. Today he was contenting himself with a cup of the vile coffee from the squad room. The odor was almost enough to make me sick. It might be better used as paint remover than for drinking.

"Don't suppose you want a cup, Peter," he said, indicating the coffee.

"I'm going to surprise you and ask for a gallon of

it," I said. "Somebody poured tar down my sinks. This stuff looks like the perfect solvent."

"Yeah, I heard the scuttlebutt about that. There's always a buzz when Satanism is involved."

"This was no teenaged prank," I said. "And it wasn't any coven of drug-crazed witches, either."

"You've got some ideas on it, you should tell the investigating officers."

"I've got the card with their phone number on it." That said nothing but he caught the tone and knew what had gone on between us. He might even have been called by the officers since I had used his name as a character witness. If he had been he wasn't going to let on.

"Been working my tail off. Got eight men out in the field asking questions of anyone they can find. Need eight more. A hundred more," he said, pawing through a stack of paper until he came to a manila folder. The size of it told me he was talking about the first body fished out of San Francisco Bay.

"What do you have?" I didn't quite trust myself. I sat rigidly in the only chair in his office and tried to force my thoughts into constructive channels. The recurring flashbacks I'd been having to the psychometry bothered me. They weren't intense but they were both unexpected and uncontrollable.

"We've got an ID on her. Seems Marcie Comstock's a model who lived over in Marin County. Nothing all that flashy, really, just a poor working stiff, if you'll excuse the expression."

"Still, Marin rents are sky-high."

"Not when you share the apartment with eight others. She and seven other models for the same agency split the costs. I figure it costs them each about three hundred a month, well within their incomes. They're all just starting out."

"What about the agency?"

Worthington shrugged. "Nothing to go on there. They give out assignments and the models usually take them. The outfit is legit. I won't bother you with a name, but it's one of the most respected in town. They do the gamut from print work to radio and television.''

"Radio?"

"Voice-overs, that kind of thing for commercials. Want a sexy voice? See them. Want a gravelly male voice? They got a library full of people able to do it. Would you believe it, they wanted to sign me up? I think they were just trying to weasel out of feeling any responsibility for their employee." Worthington sighed and went back to the report, having mentioned his one brief flirtation with fame and fortune in the entertainment world. "Mostly they do print work."

"Any runway work? Fashion modeling?"

"Some but that's not their primary arena. This is getting off the subject. I'm convinced the agency is clean. Talking with the girl's roomies makes it clear that nobody's punching a time card on who goes and who stays. As long as the pro rata share of rent is paid, nobody cares about who's sleeping there and who isn't.''

I nodded as I thought. That made sense. A model might be on call for days or weeks. An assignment might send her around the world or just down the coast. Why check in with your roommates if you didn't have to?

"Why'd they report her missing?"

"They thought it was weird she missed out on two possible jobs. And her rent was due." Worthington shrugged, as if saying it was always the money.

"Boyfriends?"

"We're working on it. It doesn't look too promising, though. She was really busting her hump at the modeling. She'd work three or four jobs to make ends meet. She knew she had to make it big in a couple years or the looks would go."

"Did she have the looks?" I asked. Worthington fished out a photo and passed it over. The woman wasn't a ravishing beauty but she did have a gamin quality that might even be called cute. As to making it into the big time, that was something I doubted would have ever happened. She didn't have "the look," whatever that was. Cindy Harrel has it, Carol Alt has it, this girl didn't.

"No boyfriends, roommates who weren't much in the way of friends—no socializing with them beyond meeting at the breakfast table for a bowl of granola— and an employer who had a couple jobs for her but she didn't show up. This is heading into a dead end, Peter. I need more to go on."

"There's nothing I can tell you, Willie. I got what I could from the anklet." I clamped my lips shut as the psychometric memories tried to force their way into my conscious mind again. The more I used the talent, the less able I was to control the adverse aspects of it. I needed something like the Rodin bronze Jena had to soothe my mind.

"I've got a box of her personal effects. I'll just let you look at the metallic stuff. That's where the best impressions are stored, right?"

"Willie . . ." Nothing was going to deter him. Settling my mind, I tried not to expose myself to the old visions fluttering across my field of vision like tuneful curtains. Already my senses were getting confused. Flutters of sound, bitter light, it was all there.

I placed my hands over a metal comb but got nothing. I went on to a hairbrush and paused. The sensations from it were more intense but still diffuse. I tried to read more into them than was there. This always spells disaster. I lost my meditative trance and came back.

"Nothing on them," I said. "Any favorite jewelry? That usually carries a more intense resonance."

"She hocked most of it, one of the roomies said. There was this, though." Worthington dropped a bracelet onto the table. A deep breath, closed eyes, deeper trance, and I found myself drifting across a misty plain staring at orange and yellow vapors rising from the bracelet.

My body turned to smoke and followed. Persimmon and cold came with the light from the bracelet. Swirling around, I felt like a compass needle, growing dizzier by the moment. When I spun around and was finally flung away, I found myself lying on the floor of Worthington's office.

"You all right, Peter? You threw yourself out of the chair. You didn't hurt yourself, did you?"

"What direction?" Scrambling to sit up, I pointed. "What direction is that?"

"North," Worthington said, not understanding.

"She had a modeling appointment to the north."

"North of what? Her apartment? San Francisco? What?"

"North," I said vaguely. It was the only impression I got. "She was excited about it because it was something different for her. She thought she might be able to make a great deal of money. She . . . she was wearing this bracelet when she took the job. I'm not sure why she left it behind."

"North, huh? Not much to go on. Maybe she got a job modeling with some outfit north of Marin. There're plenty of vineyards who do advertising."

"The bigger ones use ad agencies," I said.

"And the smaller ones might try doing it on their own."

"This isn't enough to go on, Willie. It isn't," I insisted.

"Beats what I got otherwise." He tossed the dead woman's artifacts back into the box. "I'm not even one hundred percent sure she's the one we fished out of the water, but I have to go on something."

Scissors, snip, snip, snip!

I shuddered. The psychometric memories were forcing their way back into my brain.

"I had a penknife and a tie clip passed to me on two different nights," I said, not understanding why I even brought this up. "They were the only things stolen last night."

"Your report said nothing was taken."

So he had read it.

"The officers were less than cooperative. They held me at gunpoint for what seemed an hour while they checked who I was, as if I'd burgle the place, then call and wait forty-five minutes for them to show up."

"They got there right away—less than five minutes, code two, fast driving, no lights or sirens," Worthington said.

"Their report, my reality. Anyway, I rooted around through the mess and finally saw that those were the only items missing."

"So someone passed them to you, then breaks in, trashes your place and steals them?"

"Someone steals them and then trashes the place to cover the theft," I guessed. "But I don't know why. I couldn't help feeling the power in them. I even dipped down into a light trance to really psychometrize them."

"And?"

"It was confusing. All I got was an impression of a man and scissors snipping and pain, but not the searing agony of the woman you pulled out of the Bay."

Worthington pursed his lips, then reached over and took his coffee cup. He didn't drink from it. He just clutched it as if it were a warm security blanket.

"Crazy stuff, Peter. I don't know what to tell you. I'll poke those two patrolmen a bit and get them interested. There's no way a detective will be assigned. You know that?"

"Sure, I know. There wasn't anything interesting in the vandalism."

"You go on about your business, and let me poke around to the north. I don't like it but I'm going to have to call the Chippies on this one. God, I hate that."

Worthington and the officers of the California Highway Patrol did not appreciate another's talents. They thought the SFPD was nothing but a bunch of perverted vice cops, and Worthington had often said he longed for the day when he could retire and do nothing more complicated than writing speeding tickets.

Both were wrong.

I got up and started out the door when Worthington's phone rang. He cursed under his breath and then yanked the handset from the cradle.

"What is it now? Not another murder? Damn. I'm up to my ears in corpses now. Gimme the details," he said as he pulled his well-chewed yellow pencil from behind his ear and started scribbling on a tablet in front of him.

"Yeah, yeah, a woman, late twenties. You got an ID? Well, well, this is our lucky day, isn't it? How do you spell that?"

I was closing the door when I heard Worthington repeating the name.

Jena Rosetti.

CHAPTER 15

"What's wrong?" Willie Worthington looked up from his scribbling, the phone stuck between his shoulder and his left ear. "You look like somebody just ran over your dog."

"I don't like dogs," I said automatically, stunned at what I'd just heard.

"So all right, your cat." He looked down at his notes and then back at me. "You know her? Jena Rosetti?"

A quick nod was all I could manage. I didn't really know Jena. We had met all too briefly, but something in her soul had touched me. I couldn't be sure, not now, but I think the attraction was mutual. I'd never find out for sure.

"What happened?"

"How well did you know her?"

"Was she cut in half like the other two bodies?" I didn't think I could bear that. The image of the vivacious Jena brutally slashed like a side of beef was more than anyone ought to endure.

"No, the MO's different on this one. She's not in great shape but she's not sliced and diced like the other two bodies. You can come along, if you want. Otherwise, you might wait until . . . later." Worthington finished the sentence lamely. We both knew what he had started to say. If I was so inclined, I could go to the morgue and identify the body. The notion of sitting in a sterile room and staring at a coldly flickering closed-circuit television as the attendant worked his cinematic clumsiness with the camera was almost more than I could face.

"I'd like to come along, if you don't mind."

"Let's roll," Worthington said. He grabbed the sheet of paper and tucked it away in his omnipresent notebook. "If you want, I'll buy you lunch afterward. Damn, but I'm hungry. It's this job. I never get a chance to just sit down and finish a meal." Even as he was rounding his desk, he scooped up the remains of the hot dog and stuffed it into his mouth, oblivious of the little trickle of mustard leaking down his chin. By the time we hit the squad room the yellow trickle had mysteriously vanished.

"Burnside, get your buns in gear. We got another case. This one's over in Golden Gate Park. You go on your own. Thorne's riding with me."

"What's wrong, Willie, not enough room for the three of us in your car?"

"All right, but you ride in the back."

"Hey, no, I'm—"

"Shut up, Burnie. It's either the backseat or your own car. What's it going to be?"

"I'll meet you there," the other detective said sullenly. I had never figured out if Worthington and Burnside liked each other. It didn't seem so. And I wasn't about to ask what was wrong with Worthington's rear seat. We went to the underground parking lot and got into his battered car. I had to glance into the backseat. Then I knew.

"So I need some upholstery work," Worthington said, gunning the car. "A few springs might poke out but who's to know or care? Nobody rides back there."

I settled down and stared straight ahead.

You're hurting me! Snip, cut, scissors, gush!

I shuddered as the psychometric residue forced itself into my head. Controlling it required more and more effort. Was it because I was tired or was the psychometry taking me over? The brain damage that had given me the talent had never been satisfactorily explored. Barbara Chan had tried and hit a brick wall. But the neurosurgeon who had worked on me had left the damaged portions of my brain untouched. It was dangerous meddling where nothing need be done. In a way, I'm sorry they hadn't gone in and looked for a minute obstruction, a burst vessel, a deviation from the norm, and fixed it.

Another way to keep the psychometric memories from washing over me was to isolate myself—but how was I to do that? Willie Worthington found me useful for the very reasons I was beginning to consider becoming a hermit. Could I walk away from a cold-blooded killer who sawed his victims in half and then dumped them into the Bay? My sense of justice, my need to feel that I was doing my part, prevented that. I had to help Worthington.

I had to help him destroy me. Shuddering uncontrollably, I tried to think of more pleasant things. Nothing came to me. Jena Rosetti had been killed. Since Worthington had gotten the call rather than another detective, it meant she had probably been murdered. And she had been so alive, so vibrant just the day before.

"How well did you know her?"

"What? Oh, not that well. I just met her yesterday at Gloria Gadsen's gallery."

"What are you doing hanging around a place like that? That's mighty highbrow for you, isn't it, Peter?"

"Gloria had asked me to perform. I owed her a favor."

"Ah, yes, her niece Michelle Ferris."

I keep forgetting that Worthington stores every tidbit he comes across in that vast mental storage chest of his. I'd read somewhere that the human brain has the capacity to memorize enough facts to fill the equivalent of six Bibles. Worthington's mind was stuffed with details about arrests and felons, convictions and acquittals, and people he's met casually.

"Did I mention she was Gloria's niece?" I didn't remember.

"Peter, give the old warhorse some credit. If you and

the sexy babe are going to be working together real close, I've got a duty to check up on her.''

"That's all we are. She works for me. Nothing else.''

"A shame. But you and this Jena Rosetti? That was something else?''

"I met her at the showing for a new artist's work. We talked. We hit it off. And last night she asked me to go to her place in Sausalito to examine a painting.''

"She was an art appraiser," Worthington said. "Why'd she ask you for anything? She was pretty well known. Good rep. A real pro at her work. You don't know squat about art.''

"Thanks," I said dryly. "I know a little, but you're right. She wanted me to psychometrize a painting to see if I could tell her its history. It was hard and I only got brief flashes, but it was enough to let her know she'd been taken. It was a forgery.''

"Did she know that before she called you over to examine it?''

"She suspected," I said. "There was something about it being a very good fake, though. The paint had been chipped away on one corner. What made her suspect it was counterfeit was the lack of depth. The artist hadn't painted over several other tries to get it right.''

"Strange stuff, art," Worthington said, flipping open his notebook and glancing down the page he had stuffed into it. He wrote as he drove, wobbling from side to side on the road. Other cars veered and honked at him, but Worthington was oblivious of them. We crossed Oak and hit Fell, then turned into the park. I swallowed hard when we drove past the De Young Museum. It hadn't even been twelve hours ago that Jena and I had stood outside its massive front and decided to take a short walk in the Arboretum just to the south.

"You know where the horses are exercised?" Worthington asked. He weaved in and out of traffic of JFK Drive and passed Stow Lake. "That's where she was found.''

"Recently?''

"About fifteen minutes before I got the call. She'd been dead a couple hours, or so say the forensics guys. Beaten to death. But what do they know, right?"

"I don't want to psychometrize any of her belongings, unless it's the only way to find the killer," I said.

"I understand. That's a real strain on you, isn't it?"

I closed my eyes and worked to hold back the hidden tides flowing through my brain. The dead woman, the model from Marin. The man. And mixed in with it all were the impressions from the penknife and the tie clip and even worse, Lady MacDowell and Magyar and the talk I had given this morning to the Committee to Explain the Paranormal. I almost cried out when pain hit me like a sledgehammer, and all I could see was the fake painting Jena had asked me to psychometrize. Swimming in and around and through it were Taggart's paintings, both the ones neither Jena and I cared for and the half dozen that were uniquely disturbing.

"You look like hell, Peter. You want an aspirin or something? I don't have anything stronger, unless you want some Pepto Bismol."

Sweat poured down my face. When Worthington opened the car door, the wind dried it into rivers of ice on my forehead.

"I'll be all right. I just can't seem to get everything squared away in my head."

"Look, I'm not going to ask you to do any more work on the half-'n'-half murders."

"On what?"

"That's what we're calling them. You probably haven't seen the papers. They're going even further, but that's the fourth estate for you. Or is that the fifth column? Never could keep it straight what those yahoos are supposed to do."

Worthington turned and went across a muddy field to a paved area where four large dumpsters filled with trash stood open. The police had gathered around the green dumpster on the far end. I just stood and stared. I saw Burnside drive up and park just beyond the yellow plastic tape marking the limits of the murder scene. He got out and started talking with the officers on the scene.

Worthington joined him. They stood and entered summaries of the reports into their own notebooks against the day they'd be called into court to testify. I let Worthington finish and then motion for me to come over. I didn't want to, but did, walking like a zombie, afraid of what I'd see.

"This her?" Worthington asked without preamble.

It took me a second to recognize her, but it wasn't because someone had smashed her kneecaps and turned her face to hamburger. She was dressed elegantly—fit to kill came to mind.

"Too bad a sexy broad like this has to get wasted," Burnside said. "Look at those legs. I bet they'd feel real great wr—"

"Can it, Burnside," Worthington interrupted. He stared down the other detective when Burnside started to protest. Only when Burnside was quiet did he speak to me. "Well, Peter?"

"It's Jena Rosetti," I said. In spite of the elegant dress, cut for the modern working woman on her way to the boardroom, so different from what she had worn at Gloria's gallery, I recognized the small red-and-white button incongruously pinned to her dress. She had not left her sense of humor behind when she adopted the expensive style she needed to pass chameleonlike into the world that recognized her expertise.

"We got that much from her purse. It looks like robbery, but . . ." Worthington's voice trailed off as he noted my identification in his notebook. He glanced at his watch and recorded this, too.

"She was robbed?"

"It doesn't hold up," Worthington said. "Nobody dressed to the nines like that, high heels and all, is going to be sloughing through Golden Gate Park. Look at this mud. It's been raining damned near all night. And she doesn't have a raincoat with her. No, she was killed somewhere else and dumped here."

I forced down my gorge and looked at her more closely. Her face was virtually unrecognizable because of the beating, but it was Jena. Why would anyone do this to her? I hadn't realized I'd spoken aloud until Worthington answered.

"From the looks of her legs, I'd say someone took a baseball bat to them first. Broke her knees. I've seen that before. It's mob punishment for a big mistake."

"I don't think she was supposed to croak," contributed a burly man who had been on his hands and knees behind the dumpster. He had an ME identification card clipped to the lapel on his raincoat. "The head wounds probably came after she died. She might have kicked off during the beating. The rest is just to make it look good."

"What do you mean?"

The man shrugged. Water cascaded off his yellow slicker as he moved. "She fucked up, she was punished. It'll take a full autopsy but I'll bet a week's pay that she died unexpectedly. Maybe a blood clot going from the legs into the brain. Maybe an aneurysm caused by a sudden rise in blood pressure. Something triggered by the beating, but the beating was not the proximate cause of death."

"She wouldn't have died if they hadn't beaten her like that," I protested.

"No argument on that score. I'm just saying she got roughed up and died—and that probably wasn't what the perps wanted to happen. They must have been royally pissed." He shook his head and put his hands into his pockets to keep them warm. He was getting ready to examine the body and didn't much like the idea. Still, it was his job. I was glad it wasn't mine.

I wrestled with what the forensics man had said. Jena had died accidentally? Someone had intended to cripple her for life but hadn't wanted her dead? In its perverted way, that was almost more unbelievable than her lying dead in the dumpster. What kind of beast maims but doesn't kill?

"Anything that looks as if she'd carried it around for a while?"

"Not really, Sergeant. The obvious stuff—jewelry, money, credit cards—were all removed from her purse. She had a couple slips of paper which ID'd her."

"You have any idea who she was working for, Peter?"

"She wouldn't say. You might go through her houseboat over in Sausalito. She must have kept financial records showing her employers. Maybe at her bank will be a listing of deposits. All the banks microfilm everything coming through these days."

Worthington laughed harshly. "Her job was to buy stuff for people who didn't want to be traced. She worked in cash. Chances are pretty good that she didn't declare ten percent of what she really made a year. She's probably a prime candidate for a tax evasion rap—or would have been if it hadn't been for this."

"There's got to be some way to trace her employer." Again I didn't realize I was speaking aloud. The distant roar of the ocean confused me, filling my head with white noise and making it easier for the repressed psychometrized memories to sneak back.

Death, always death and pain, misery and suffering.

"We'll ask around, but they're a secretive breed, those art collectors," Worthington said. "I remember when I was first promoted to detective, I had a case where one of the fancy-ass houses up on Nob Hill was burgled. A real pro job. Never saw anything slicker in all my years on the force. The owner wouldn't cop to anything. Nothing stolen, he said. He was lying through his teeth and we both knew it. I did some digging. He was one of the biggest buyers of stolen artwork on the West Coast."

"Did you ever get any of the artwork back?" I asked.

Worthington shook his head. "I figure the art was stolen for another of the anonymous megabucks guys. It's probably still hanging in some secret basement with special lights, for the appreciation of one or two people.''

"Do you figure she was raped first?" Burnside asked.

I jerked around and stared at him. The question was entirely malicious on his part. I hadn't seen any evidence that Jena had been sexually assaulted. While her austere business dress had been soiled with her blood and with the garbage in the dumpster, it was relatively untorn.

"Burnside, I'm putting you in for asshole of the year. For a while there it looked like Booth or Wilson might give you a run for your money, but after this one, hell, they'll just have to fold up and wait till next year." Worthington frowned hard at the other detective, who only sneered. I didn't know why he hated me so much, but he obviously did.

Burnside wandered off to do who knows what. I didn't care whether it was productive, so long as it got him away from me.

"A real jerk. Try not to mind him too much," Worthington said. "You have any hint at all about who she was working for? I take it her boss wasn't pleased, and he was the one who did this."

I said nothing. The same thought had been running through my mind. Jena had mentioned her employer several times. She been careful not to give me any clue to his identity—but I had the distinct impression it was a "he" rather than a "she." I didn't think Jena would have been as frightened of a woman.

"Hell of an employer. No need for a retirement plan. I doubt his employees live long enough," I said.

"The kneecaps. I keep coming back to that," mused Worthington. "Mob stuff. I think her mysterious employer was connected. You have any way of getting a handle on it?"

"I'll try," I said, thinking hard. Gloria Gadsen might know, and she might tell me things she wouldn't dare disclose to Worthington. The rich bought far more paintings from her gallery than the poor. She didn't dare blow the whistle on anyone, even a gangster. From what Michelle had said, the gallery wasn't doing as well as I'd thought. This might make Gloria even more reluctant to talk.

But she would to me. Jena Rosetti was nothing but a passing acquaintance, but I felt poorer for not having known her better. The forensics man finished his examination of the body and pushed free of the garbage. He motioned to the silent team to come over and bag the body. I watched in frozen appreciation of the care and speed they showed. I was glad Burnside wasn't doing this.

"Got this, Sergeant," the man said, passing two small plastic bags to Worthington. "Caught in her dried blood, one on her kneecap and the other on her right hand. She might have batted at the killer. Or maybe it's only a dog hair. The lab boys will have to do the workup to be sure of what's here."

Worthington held them up to the gray sky. I got a good look at the contents. In one envelope was a dark hair. The bright red hair in the other seemed out of place among Jena's mousy brown. But did either belong to her murderer?

CHAPTER 16

I sat in Willie Worthington's office, mulling over everything that had happened. The world was in chaos and it was sucking me into its vortex. Jena Rosetti dead.

The pain! Don't do it to me! Please!

The odors rising from the pain assaulted my nose and made it drip. When I reached up to wipe it, I found that it was perfectly dry. It had only been a psychometric memory confusing my senses. I closed my eyes and put myself into a light trance, thinking I might be able to sort through the jungle of sensations forcing themselves on me. It didn't work—quite.

"What's wrong, Peter?" came a distant voice.

"Everything is jumbled," I murmured, not wanting to break concentration but needing to reply. Worthington would call a paramedic if it looked like I was slipping into a coma. "I need it ordered. I need to keep it straight in my head."

"I've got some aspirin," he offered. This seemed to be his remedy for everything.

The trance slid past me and I rose, drifting on top of it like a cork on the ocean and coming out of the otherworldly astral plane where psychometry is possible. I left behind the welter of haunting memories without coming to any conclusions. The answer was so close and yet it eluded me—perhaps I just *thought* the answer was there. Too many variables kept me off balance mentally. Too many events and too many deaths.

"You look like homemade shit," Worthington said, using one of his favorite descriptions.

"I feel like it. There's something I'm missing and I don't know how to reach it."

"Like an itch in the middle of your back?"

"In the middle of my brain," I said. Glancing at my watch, I cursed under my breath. Time was speeding up or I was slowing down. There never seemed to be enough of it to do everything I had to. "Let me use your phone. I need to call Michelle Ferris and cancel our rehearsal. I should have been at the theater hours ago. She'll think I skipped town rather than go onstage with her."

This somewhat frivolous statement proved all to accurate. Michelle was in tears, thinking I had forsaken her. I told her something of what had happened and why I was still at the police station, then said, "I'll be at the theater in time for the show. You go through the book again and make sure you've got everything down pat."

"Peter, there's something I need to tell you."

"When I get to the theater. I've still got a couple of places to go before work." I didn't give her a chance to go on. Michelle had reacted worse than I'd've thought.

"What are you going to do?" Worthington was in his familiar pose, feet on the desk and his chewed yellow pencil firmly tucked behind his right ear.

"What you ought to be doing," I said, perhaps a bit too harshly. "I want to find out who Jena's employer was."

"The one she bought the fake painting for? Yeah, that's a good place to start. I've only got a couple men on it."

"What about those detectives on the, uh, half-'n'-half murderers, as you called them?"

"So my squad is spread thin. Real thin. That's why I'm not saying you should butt out. The truth is, Peter, you make a better cop than most of them out there."

Burnside's raucous laughter echoed into the office. Worthington snorted in contempt. "Take Burnie. You make him look like a buffoon. He'll never learn to ask the right questions—and when to keep his mouth shut and just listen.''

"He doesn't like me," I said. "That's all right. I don't much like him, either.''

"Where are you heading? I might be able to give you a lift.''

"I'm not going far," I said. Gloria Gadsen's gallery wasn't more than ten blocks away. I could walk it faster than I could drive. The day had slipped away, what with the morning lecture and Jena's death. It was a little before six. I had to get to the Rialto and prepare for my show at eight, but the lure of finding out who Jena's boss had been edged out my better judgment.

"So don't go far, and don't get into trouble doing it. I ought to be getting a report back from up north on any possible modeling jobs the first corpse might have taken.''

"North," I muttered, the vague whispers coming back to me over the not-so-subtle accompaniment of pain. It was as if a dozen people tried to crowd into my skull at the same time. There was hardly room for me in there, much less the Greek chorus telling me things I didn't want to hear.

I hurried out of Worthington's office and crossed Market, dodging trolleys and the heavy rush-hour traffic. I must have gotten to Gloria's shop just as it closed. The blinds were drawn on the door. Checking the windows, I saw a small sign saying the gallery was only open until 5:30. I'd missed her by more than a half hour.

I'd have to catch her later, or perhaps I could get her home number from Michelle and call just before the show started.

I turned to go up the steps and back to street level when I heard noises inside the gallery. My heart leaped in my chest. I could get my information now and not have to wait. Knocking hard on the door, I called out, "This is Peter. I need to talk to you, Gloria.''

The rapping didn't get a response.

"Marie? Gloria? This will take only a few minutes. I've got to go soon." I listened hard but the sounds had died out. There wasn't any way Gloria or Marie could have missed my insistent knocking. My voice might have been drowned out if they were at the rear of the gallery but the sharp beating on the door would have roused the dead. Then the thought hit me that if they were where they couldn't hear me at the door, then I shouldn't have been able to hear them.

It was also possible that they didn't want to talk to me. I decided to press the matter and do a little exploring. I wasn't quite sure where the service entrance to the gallery was, but it couldn't be too far.

Maiden Lane is only a couple of blocks long and it is closed to vehicular traffic. I went to the cross street and turned north until I came to the service alley. Just as I rounded the corner and started down the alley to find the rear door, a white panel ruck gunned its engine and exploded from the alley. My quick reflexes saved me. I dived into a pile of rubbish, burrowing hard into the garbage under it. I felt the hot exhaust from the truck as it screeched around the corner and went north. Shaking off the debris, I ran back to the corner. The truck was already out of sight. It might have turned the next corner and gone over to Jones or Taylor.

Disgusted at such lousy driving, I continued brushing off the garbage. My nose twitched as I got the largest pieces off. My clothing was irretrievably stained. I was getting down to my last suit of street clothing. Sooner or later I'd have to go shopping. And it was going to have to be soon. Even my shoes squished from the liquid waste I'd tromped through.

I came to the Gadsen Gallery's back door. It didn't take a twenty-year veteran beat cop to see that the door had been jimmied. Compared to the job done on my apartment door, this was a crude job, but effective. I examined the dead bolts and changed my opinion of it being a hasty job. Whoever had ripped open the steel-plated door had been more expert than that. Only the minimum amount of force had been used to get the door open. No wasted energy here.

Another thought hit me. There ought to be burglar alarms going off everywhere. I didn't hear a sound, other than the normal street background. I entered slowly, wondering if Gloria had a silent alarm installed.

Looking around the gallery didn't tell me a great deal. The lights were low, and I had come in on the level of Gloria's office. Being careful, I made my way through the office. Nothing had been touched. I wondered if I was letting myself in for a world of trouble. The notion that Gloria had a silent alarm that was even now bringing down hordes of police kept flashing through my mind. But I ascribed it to an overactive imagination. It didn't *feel* right.

The spiral staircase down into the gallery itself wasn't lighted. I descended into darkness. Faint key lights showed over empty walls. I wondered if it was supposed to be this way. A quick tour of the gallery showed more than a dozen of Taggart's paintings gone. Gloria had sold quite a few.

I couldn't help noticing the ones that had affected me so strongly were gone. This didn't mean much. They had caught Jena Rosetti's attention, too, and no doubt others at the exhibition had also been drawn by their savage genius. Once more I stopped and stared at the other paintings Taggart had done, the ones that lacked the flair, the fervor, the intensity of *Maelstrom of Disquiet* and *Subway to the Soul* and the other two.

I was left curiously unaffected. Why should four produce such powerful emotions and the rest of the man's work be . . . nothing? I felt as if a great secret of the universe was at hand. What made genius and what made for merely competent work? The muse of artists had touched Taggart a few times and no more.

Shrugging it off, I checked the storerooms. They were empty. Returning to the stairs, I bounded up, taking them two at a time. A glance at the phone told me where my duty lay. I dialed the police and reported the break-in, then punched the autodial button next to Gloria's name.

"What is it?" came the querulous question.

"Gloria?"

"Yes, is that you, Peter?"

"I'm at your store. I had hoped to catch you here, but—"

"I'm sorry you missed me. I've had such a headache all day. I didn't even come to work this morning. Marie ran the store."

"She's not here."

"She'd have closed at five-thirty," Gloria paused, then asked, "How did you get my home number? It's not listed. Did you get it from Michelle?"

"I used the auto-dialer on your desk phone. When I came by I heard noises inside. You've been robbed."

"Peter, no!"

"I called the police. You'd better get down here to vouch for me. I look like a street person right now. I'll explain it all." Sirens sounded outside. The alley would be blocked off at both ends. It's nice running a high-profile business in the heart of San Francisco business district not five blocks from a precinct station. I'd had to wait forty-five minutes to get a patrol car out; Gloria's name brought them running.

The first thing I saw was the muzzle of a service revolver coming through the door.

"In here, Officer. I called a few minutes ago." From there it was a repeat of the other night. They searched me, doubted me, and would have run me in except that they took long enough in searching the premises and in asking pointless questions that Gloria Gadsen showed up.

"Peter, are you all right? You look a mess!"

"It's always nice to be admired for my sartorial skills," I said dryly. "I was almost run over by the crooks as they escaped."

"Why the hell didn't you say so, mister?" demanded

a uniformed officer. "They must have gotten away by now."

"A long time ago, actually," I said glancing at a designer clock on Gloria's office wall. It was hard to believe but I had been inside for over fifteen minutes. The time had flashed by when examining Taggart's work.

"Why are you so filthy?" asked Gloria. I saw the officer begin writing down my responses.

"The white van that came out of the alley tried to run me down. I dived into a pile of garbage." I looked down and wrinkled my nose. I was starting to get fragrant.

"Get a license on the truck?"

"All I got was a blast of hot air as it went by. I was lucky not to have its grill in place of my teeth."

"What about the driver?"

I shook my head. I hadn't noticed. Saving my own skin had been too big a priority at the time to step aside coolly and remember what the driver looked like. I wasn't even sure that had been a passenger in the van.

"You'll vouch for him, Ms. Gadsen?"

"Don't be ridiculous, Officer, of course I will. He's an old and dear friend."

"I didn't hear an alarm when I found the door open," I said. "Don't you have one?"

"Of course, I do. Marie must not have set it, the foolish girl."

"No, ma'am, it wasn't like that," said another officer. "We checked it. Somebody had filled it full of shaving cream. It was ringing to beat the band but the foam deadened the sound. A few feet away you'd never notice it."

"Oh, my." Gloria sat down suddenly. "What did they take, Peter?"

This startled me. I hadn't been expecting to need an inventory.

"Some of Taggart's pieces are still hanging. I don't

know which ones you'd sold and which you hadn't. There's no way I could tell you—''

"Over half were sold," Gloria said, "but their owners weren't supposed to pick them up until after the exhibit closed on Friday.''

"So if there's a blank spot on the wall, that means a missing painting?" asked the officer. He glanced over his shoulder when a short, hunched-over man entered. A gold detective's badge gleamed where it hung from the man's coat pocket. The uniform left off interrogating us and went to give what he had to the detective.

I took the chance to grab Gloria's elbow and get her out of the chair. "Let's check down below before they start asking questions," I said. "You'd know better than I could what's gone.''

She started crying when she saw the large empty spaces on the walls.

"I'm ruined, Peter. The paintings were sold but they weren't insured. I sold over three-quarters of a million dollars of Taggart's paintings—and they're all gone!''

"Not all of them," I said. "Whoever robbed you has been selective. Why leave these three by the stairs but take four at the rear of the gallery? Paintings are paintings.''

"You're right. All these were sold. I . . . I won't have to make good on them." Gloria wiped the tears away and started through the winding panels to take a quick inventory against the catalogue of Taggart's work.

I followed, trying to remember which paintings were gone and if Jena had said anything about them. It was a fool's task. I found myself getting memories of the woman mixed up with her opinions of the paintings.

"It's bad, Peter. The thieves took the best of the collection. They were all sold. Or most were.''

"But the thieves didn't take all that were sold?''

"No, not really. A few of the unsold ones are still here, but a couple I hadn't been able to sell are gone. The thieves were very selective in what they stole.''

That made sense if a collector was out to add to his

Taggart collection. Come to the showing, make the want list, and then send a couple burglars around to do your shopping. It was efficient and cold-blooded.

"What about the ones Clarke Yancey bought?"

"I don't know. Let's see. There's one of his and over there." Gloria frowned as she worked to remember. "The others he bought are gone. Two are left, four— no, five—were taken."

That made no sense to me if Yancey was responsible for the heist. He didn't seem like the subtle kind. He'd steal all the ones he had contracted to buy so he wouldn't be out a dime and would still have the paintings. Why take only a fraction when he would still be on the hook for the two the thieves had left?

"Is he likely to try to back out because five of the seven are gone?"

"Possibly, but I don't think so. Remember how I sold them."

Gloria's words sparked the memory and the accompanying coldness in my gut. I remembered. Yancey ought to have been hauled off to jail for what he tried to do to Michelle.

"Was there anyone else who showed interest but didn't buy any of Taggart's paintings?"

"Yeah, Ms. Gadsen, that's a real good question. I'm hoping you've got a real good answer so we can wrap this up quick." The short detective had come down the spiral staircase. I'd been too engrossed to notice until he spoke.

"There's no one I can think of," Gloria said. "The paintings weren't insured. This is a horrible loss."

"Is that usual business for you, not to insure?"

"Business hasn't been good lately," Gloria admitted. "I'd hoped to get a little ahead and—"

"And so you cut corners. Who's on the hook for the value of the paintings, you or the artist?"

"Taggart," she said. "The standard gallery release he signed says we assume no responsibility for the paintings."

"So it's this guy Taggart who's been burned by the theft and not you?" The detective scowled and began writing in a slow, curlicue style that filled page after page.

"The standard release?" I had to ask. "You mean this is the way it's usually done?"

Gloria nodded. "The artist assumes all responsibility for the paintings, even though the gallery is displaying them. I doubt if Taggart had them insured."

"Will you have to pay him for the missing pieces?" The entire gallery business seemed more incredible than words.

"No, Peter. And I'm so grateful that not all the sold pieces were stolen. This will help my cash flow."

"What's the usual break, Ms. Gadsen? How much does the artist get and how much do you take as gallery owner?" The detective's pen was poised over the page, waiting for the answer.

"We take sixty percent. He gets forty."

"Taggart's the big loser all around, isn't he?" I said. I hadn't realized galleries took such a large portion of the artist's money—and forced him to assume the risk without even going partners on insurance against possible loss.

"Yes, but there are losses other than money involved," Gloria said. "When this gets out, it may be impossible for me to attract other artists of Taggart's caliber. The gallery suffers, even if you get the paintings back."

"I don't want to lead you on about this, Ms. Gadsen." The detective cleared his throat and looked at her squarely. "We don't have much to go on. A white van and that's about it. There're hundreds of them in San Francisco. Without your, uh, friend getting a look at the plates, we're not even sure the van is registered in California."

"You'll dust the place for prints, won't you?"

"Sure, but it won't do much good. The uniforms saw the entry point. They said it was a real pro job. A pair of gloves is all the thieves would need to conceal their identities. Somebody might have seen someone tinkering with the exterior alarm, but I don't really think we're going to break the case that way.''

''Who would notice anything down an alley during rush hour that they'd be willing to report?'' I said.

''Something like that. We'll need a list of everything taken, and photographs of the paintings. I'll turn it over to the Fine Arts Division.''

''There's a division that handles art thefts?''

''All sorts of things like this. Art forgery, theft, numismatic crimes, some bunco—they're experts on artwork.'' The detective shrugged. ''Unless somebody tries to fence a piece and we have a good photo, I don't hold much hope for getting any of the stuff back.'' He peered at one of Taggart's pieces still on the wall. ''There's nothing distinctive about this. I mean it's not a picture of a mountain or a horse or anything.''

''The others were about the same,'' Gloria said, understanding what the detective meant.

''So, get us the photos. You *do* have photographs of the pieces?''

''Yes, for the program guide,'' Gloria said, indicating the brochure she had in her hand. ''I'll go through the exhibit and check what's still hanging.''

''Get it to me over at the precinct,'' the detective said. ''Here's my card. Or you can just bump it over to Fine Arts. They're on the same floor.''

The detective whistled for the forensics team. The two, a man and woman, came down the stairs and worked quickly to dust wherever a print might be placed by a careless burglar.

''We'll need to fingerprint you and all your employees. And anyone who's been in here since the last time you cleaned. That includes janitors, cleaning women, maintenance types, the whole lot of them. We need to establish which prints don't belong and which do.''

''This isn't going to accomplish a thing. There was a public display,'' Gloria said. ''After the invitation-only showing, anyone could have come in and left prints.''

"I'm just doing my job," he said almost defensively. "I was giving it to you straight when I told you there's not much chance to getting the paintings back." He scowled and asked, "They *are* paintings? They look sorta strange. Oils?''

"They're paintings," Gloria said. "Acrylics mostly, with some gouache. That's a technique using opaque watercolors," she explained quickly, as much for my benefit as for his. "Taggart uses both brush and air-brush to achieve the depth and—''

"That's okay," the detective said. "I understand air-brush and watercolor and even acrylic. There's not much more I do understand, though.'' He finished writing with a flourish and went to badger the forensics crew.

"Oh, Peter, why did this have to happen now of all times? I was just getting back on my feet financially. This is going to make it hard to keep the business going.''

I hated to interrogate her further, but a few missing paintings were nothing compared with Jena Rosetti's murder. The excitement had preempted my original reason for seeking Gloria out, but now it came roaring back to the forefront of my thoughts.

"Do you know who Jena Rosetti worked for?''

"What? Jena? She works for several people, but she was always secretive about it. Those kind of people always are. It's a sacred trust with them—and they'd never get any work if just anyone knew who they were buying for.''

"You don't have any idea who she was buying for? Who might have hired her to look at paintings?''

"Not really. Collectors willing to spend real money don't want to announce everything they have in their private hoards. If someone makes a large bid at an auction and is recognized, well, that's asking to be robbed.''

"Did she mention a painting she'd purchased recently that might be a forgery?"

"No, we seldom talked about such things. She was a very good appraiser and had an eye for value. Jena had no reason to ask my opinion on any of her acquisitions. It surprises me to think she would be taken in by a forgery. It would have to be a damned good one. As I said, Jena has a good eye."

Gloria stared at me curiously. "What's the sudden interest in her?" She smiled as she thought she came to the right conclusion. "I saw the way you two hit it off at the showing yesterday. Do you want her phone number? She lives over in Sausalito, I believe. I'd have to get it out of my files."

"That's all right," I said. "Even if I called, there wouldn't be anyone home."

Ever again.

CHAPTER 17

"Is everything going okay, Peter? I can't tell, and I'm so nervous." Michelle shifted from one foot to the other. We were taking a brief break while the stage-hands cleared the way for the last big act of the show. I had decided to skip the mentalist portion of the act tonight, though it might have been interesting in a twisted way to see if the people who had broken into my apartment and trashed it so thoroughly might not pass back the penknife and tie clip just to taunt me.

"Going fine," I said. "Look, if there's anyone to blame for anything that's happened tonight, it's on my shoulders."

"I'm supposed to follow your lead," Michelle said, tugging anxiously at her costume. "I'm still so new at this."

"I'd wanted to rehearse this afternoon," I said, "but everything got in the way."

She looked at me, her bright blue eyes wide and innocent. "I hadn't wanted to say anything, but why were your clothes so filthy? It looked as if you'd been rooting around in the garbage."

"I had," I said, looking through the small hole in the curtain to study the crowd. Perhaps I would see a familiar face and identify whoever had passed me the two items stolen from my apartment. I saw a few people I recognized, but they were old friends who knew I wasn't going to be performing at the Rialto much longer. In fact, if the quality of tonight's performance was any indication, Barry Morgan might just decide not to wait to end my run here.

I hadn't been able to concentrate fully on my work. Michelle had tried to cover one or two of my gaffes, but she lacked the experience to do it well. If anything, she had pointed out the mistakes to the audience rather than covering them. I couldn't fault her for trying; I could only blame myself for not taking the time to rehearse more with her and for not being in top form. The crowd at the Rialto deserved my best performance even if Morgan merited only my lowest opinion.

The finale was a variation on the man-in-the-oven trick popular in the thirties. Michelle opened the door of the specially prepared cabinet and showed the meat hanging on hooks. I lit the fire, actually nothing more than alcohol-soaked rags. The flames looked devastating and the smell of cooking meat—reheated meat, actually—wafted to the front rows and made them sure the meat was cooking in the leaping flames. Then I put out the fire and Michelle crawled into the oven.

I spun the apparatus around and lit the fires again. Just enough of the top showed so that the hanging meat was seen. I walked around the cabinet and quickly exchanged places with her where she was sequestered in a small space under the flames, breathing through a rubber tube.

"Careful," I said as I jumped up on a hidden peg so my feet vanished from sight. "Your feet can be seen if you move over just a few inches." Designing the trick so that it was possible to walk around and be out of sight for just a fraction of a second was easier than it seemed. I slid in and pulled the door shut. Michelle dropped down and walked out to appear at the far side of the cabinet. We had taken less than three seconds to make the switch. To the audience captivated by the roasting meat, it had seemed far less.

She finished the act by extinguishing the flames and throwing open the oven. I sat inside picking my teeth, apparently roasting but oblivious of the heat. The truth was that the worst of the heat came from the spotlights. The alcohol-fed fires were relatively cool.

But the illusion was finished. Michelle and I took our bows and left the stage.

"That was a good one, the oven bit," Barry Morgan said. "What you want to do with the meat inside?"

"Give it to some kitchen for the homeless," I said. "That's what I always do."

"I'll see to it."

I started to protest, then saw that Michelle had been called to the phone. She turned and stared at me with eyes that mirrored both stark fear and a hint of something more. "Do what you want to with it," I said to Morgan. He rubbed his hands together like Ebenezer Scrooge and went off to lay claim to the meat. He was probably going to sell it, but I was more occupied with Michelle than with the theater manager.

"What's wrong?" I asked her.

"You didn't tell me you were almost killed this afternoon. That was Aunt Gloria. She said you, she, her gallery, oh! Peter, what's going on? This is all too much for me!"

"Come into my dressing room," I said, glancing around. Michelle was attracting the attention of the stagehands. They were insatiable gossips. I didn't want my part in the gallery robbery getting around. I felt it had something to do with Jena Rosetti's death—and in some gut-level way, that it tied in with the problems I'd been having. The trashed apartment, the grisly penknife and tie clip, maybe even the two murders on which Worthington had asked me for help.

"Why didn't you tell me?" she asked again.

"There wasn't that much time before the show, and I didn't want to worry you. You seem to have trouble coping with things like this." I didn't even bother going into Jena's death. Michelle was distraught enough over the robbery and the notion I'd been so close to catching the thieves.

"Aunt Gloria said you were magnificent. She said you handled yourself well and you saw the thieves driving off in a truck."

"They almost drove over me, and I didn't get a chance to see them." I wondered if they might have dropped a clue that I could psychometrize. It didn't seem likely. They were too accomplished; they had known exactly what they wanted and how best to get it.

"I don't know if I can keep on much longer, Peter. Things are so, so confused for me. The troubles. I shouldn't bother you with this."

I heard the approaching mental derailment and did my best to calm her. The details of her trouble back East had never been fully revealed. She had given me enough facts, and Gloria had hinted at enough others, to make me think Michelle had spent a considerable amount of time trying to piece together her life. Gloria wanted to protect her and at the same time let her get on with her life.

"Do you remember Jena Rosetti?" I asked, skirting the matter of the woman's death.

"The mousy girl at the showing? Yes, I do. We talked a little while you were in the back room with Aunt Gloria."

"Did Jena happen to mention who she was working for? She put in a bid on one of Taggart's paintings."

"She said she was going to bid on several of them," Michelle replied. "I don't know which ones. You think she had something to do with the robbery?"

"Not directly, but I'm wondering about the person she was buying for." This wasn't exactly a lie, but it was definitely verbal sleight of hand. Michelle would find out about Jena Rosetti's murder sooner or later. I preferred it to be later. Now, I needed information she might have without the curtains of fright and anxiety she was likely to pull up at the mention of a killing.

Michelle frowned as she chewed on her lower lip and tried to remember. "She mentioned working for someone a couple times, but she never said who. I had the feeling, though, her employer was at the showing."

"What makes you say that?"

"Just the way she'd study a painting, then look over her shoulder, as if waiting for a signal. Or maybe she was signaling someone that she had found one she liked and needed approval."

That didn't sound too likely to me. On the other hand, neither did someone killing Jena because she had bought a forgery. A quarter of a million wasn't chicken feed, but it was far from being a total disaster for someone able to hire an expert to do their art purchasing anonymously. There were risks in every business. Jena's unknown employer had to be aware of the risk he ran.

"You don't have any idea who it was she was looking to for approval?"

Michelle shook her head. Before I could press the issue and see if I could shake loose some small detail she might have forgotten, there was a knock at my door. I heaved myself to my feet and went to see what Morgan wanted. To my surprise no one was there. Even the stagehands had made themselves scarce.

As I turned to go back into my dressing room, my foot kicked a small package on the floor. I picked it up. Simple brown twine had been wrapped around a tiny parcel.

"For you?" I asked Michelle, holding it out for her. I couldn't think of anyone who would send me a present.

"Who's it from?"

"There's no card. Maybe it's from one of my legion of admirers." I grinned crookedly as I put the small package onto my dressing table. "If that's the case, I might call the bomb squad first."

"It's too small for a bomb," Michelle said. "Do you want me to open it?"

"Go on." I started getting the makeup off my face. It always tightened my skin and made me feel years older. The relief that came from washing the final bit off is almost indescribable. As I worked I tried to formulate my next question to Michelle about Jena's employer.

"I don't understand," she said. "Maybe it is from an admirer. But you'd have to know her."

"Her?"

Michelle handed me a single key. I turned it over and over in my hand.

"I don't understand, either. It's not to any lock I know." Through long years in stage magic, I've learned to run my fingers over the notches in a key and "memorize" them. When blindfolded, I can pick the proper key for the appropriate lock during escapes. I might have a dozen keys to go through. If I am sealed in an airtight container, it helps to be able to recognize keys in several ways.

I closed my eyes and worked on a light trance. Psychometrizing wasn't something I ought to do without full consideration of the psychic penalties, but I did it anyway. I wanted to know who had left the key on my doorstep.

"Peter?"

"It's all right," I said, uneasy at the vibrations I picked up from the key. There was an odor, a perfume, that mixed beauty and death. The swirling curtains of mist that I plowed through to find the odors told me nothing about the key's owner. Small sounds had popped up for me to examine, but I didn't recognize them, either. "I don't know whose key this is, but it's from a woman."

"You can really tell that? Amazing."

I shrugged it off. I needed to know more about Jena's employer. The key and who had left it were minor mysteries that might never be solved. I had the feeling that I could do something important in tracking down Jena's murderer.

"Do you think Gloria kept a list of all her invited guests?"

Michelle laughed. "Aunt Gloria is a pack rat. She files everything away. I'm sure she does."

"Did she call you from her home?"

"I suppose so. Yes, she must have. She said she had a teapot on the stove and had to go tend it."

"I suppose I'd better stop by her place and ask. Do you think she'd mind if I dropped by?"

"What? No, I don't see why she would," Michelle said uncertainly. I hated to push her but I knew her weaknesses and capitalized on them.

"What's the address again? I don't seem to remember it. You said she wouldn't mind."

"No, she wouldn't. I don't think," Michelle said, even less sure of herself. Then she was pushed over the edge into decision by me standing up. I towered over her, dominating her with my presence. She couldn't turn me down when I handed her paper and pencil to write down the address for me.

Gloria Gadsen had never given me her home phone number, much less her address for some reason. She probably valued her privacy. I know I did mine. When you're in the public eye, even as an art gallery owner, all kinds of weirdos show up at your door if you're not careful.

Michelle left to go to her own dressing room, and I tucked the paper with Gloria's address away into the fold of my jacket. I didn't have any street clothing left worth mentioning. I'd have to go wearing my stage costume. But it was not going to draw any undue attention at this time of night.

I hefted the mysterious key that had been left, then slid it into a small Velcro-fastened pocket on my sleeve. I had more important things to worry about and hoped Gloria could help me with them.

CHAPTER 18

I had to use my street map twice to find Gloria Gadsen's house. She lived in a cul-de-sac just off Masonic and to the east of Golden Gate Park. It wasn't far from the Haight-Ashbury district, not the kind of place I'd expect a successful art gallery owner to live. But then Gloria had said she'd been having financial difficulties.

As I drove around the loop, it occurred to me that she might have lived here for many years. The entire neighborhood looked well established, as though the people who lived there did not move around very much. I can understand having roots and being unwilling to prune them, even if you come into some upscale dollars.

I parked my BMW and got out, searching for the house number. The lack of good lighting had betrayed my eyes. I had misread a number and had parked around the bend in the loop from Gloria's house. The stuccoed fronts looked similar, and I was going carefully to be sure I didn't disturb someone at the wrong house when I saw the black limo parked along the far curb. It was so totally out of character for what I took to be a stodgy middle-class neighborhood that I stopped and stared.

A red-haired man in a chauffeur's uniform leaned against the right fender, arms crossed and looking toward a house with a neatly painted exterior. It didn't take an Einstein to figure out he was watching the front door to Gloria's house.

Several possibilities occurred to me, but I didn't much like any of them. I decided to do an end run rather than confront the gorilla of a driver directly. His truculent expression as he turned and looked around told me he was stationed there to keep away intruders.

The houses were built one wall against another, a sort of early-day town house arrangement. The only difference was that two walls had been used rather than having the houses share in the construction. I retraced my steps and got back out onto the main street. It took five minutes to find the alley running behind Gloria's house. I opened the white-painted wooden gate into her backyard cautiously and walked almost gingerly to her back door. If any of the neighbors saw me, they'd be sure to report a Peeping Tom.

That might be for the best. From inside the house I heard loud voices, an argument, shouts, and then a shrill scream.

Taking the time to go next door and call the police was the prudent thing to do. It might also give whoever was inside time to kill Gloria Gadsen. I tested the old-style cut-glass doorknob and rattled it twice. Gloria had secured it against anyone sneaking in from the alley.

But I wasn't just any burglar. I picked the lock within seconds and climbed the back staircase leading up to the main part of her house. The voices were louder now. Gloria screamed again.

"Shut up, bitch," came the cold words. "You can screech all you want when you give me what I want."

"Get out of here, Pickering. I told you the truth. There's nothing I can do."

"I could sue but that takes too long. You could tie everything up in court for years. I want it all now. Now, dammit, you conniving bitch."

"Get the hell out of my house."

Gloria screamed again, but this time it was a shriek of pain rather than indignation. I took the steps three at a time and got to her kitchen. Looking through the small area, I saw Roy Pickering standing over her. His hand was cocked back as if he was going to slap her. I saw Gloria's legs kicking futilely. Pickering had her pinned down and was going to hit her.

"Don't do this," Gloria pleaded.

"You're trying to double-cross me. I don't like that. Give me what I want and I'll get the fuck out of here."

"I ca—"

Gloria never got the chance to answer. Roy Pickering hit her. Hard. I saw Gloria's head snap back and her eyes roll up in her head. He hadn't just slapped her. He had balled his fist and struck her as hard as he could.

He didn't get a second chance. I know better than to hit someone with my fist. That's a good way of breaking bones. I measured the distance, took three quick steps, and launched a powerful kick that ended on Pickering's chin.

The man sagged as if he were a marionette with its strings cut. He fell off of her and lay sprawled on the floor, moaning and trying to shake his head clear. He wasn't going to be a problem for several minutes. I checked on Gloria.

"Are you all right?" I asked. I rubbed her cheek where Pickering had struck her. The bruise was already forming. Gloria's eyes came into a slow focus. At first she stared at me as if she didn't see me; then it was as if she didn't recognize me.

"Peter?"

The words were slurred. I didn't think her jaw was broken, but I'm no doctor.

"Don't talk, Gloria. I'll take care of him."

"Wait, no, this is all right, Peter."

I didn't let her get any further. Roy Pickering was stirring and beginning to mumble louder and louder. He was trying to call his driver. Pickering was not that hard to deal with. He was a slight man who didn't look as if he kept in very good shape, but his chauffeur was another matter. That one was the kind who crushed billiard balls in his fists for the hell of it.

I dropped, putting my knee squarely into his gut. The air whooshed out of him, and he started gasping for air like a beached fish.

"This isn't as much fun as beating up a woman, is

it, Pickering? Don't try calling your goon outside or I'll stuff your tongue down your throat until you can lap at your own asshole.''

"Thorne," he grunted out. The air was gusting back into his tortured lungs. "I'll kill you for this." He struggled to his feet, supporting himself against a counter.

"Don't make promises you can't keep."

I wasn't expecting him to try anything more, but the fight still hadn't left him. He swung clumsily with his left hand, trying to land his palm against my ear and deafen me. I ducked down and blocked the blow with my right arm. Then I drove my palm squarely into his nose. Blood spurted as the nose broke.

Pickering let out a howl of pain and jerked away. My coat sleeve caught on his watch. He kept thrashing around and spraying blood everywhere and I felt my sleeve ripping. It was inevitable so I let him do it. My costume was ruined on two counts. If the blood didn't make it look as if I worked in a slaughterhouse, then the torn sleeve would make it unfit for use in my act.

"I'll sue you for everything you've got," the lawyer kept saying over and over as he tried to stop the bleeding. By this time Gloria had regained her senses. She rubbed her jaw and went over to Pickering. She faced him down.

"Try to sue and I'll have you up on charges. It's not enough that your client tried to rape my niece. Now you've got to go around beating up old women. How will that look when you're pulled up on ethics charges in front of the state Bar?''

"This is a frame. You'll never get away with it, either of you." Roy Pickering edged toward the door, his nose still dripping blood everywhere. I took no satisfaction in punching his lights out. The adrenaline rush had passed, and I now just hoped he didn't get his driver to come in and give me what I had given him.

"And I'll get those pictures if it's the last thing I ever do. You'll see me in court, you old cu—''

I didn't let him finish. I took two more steps and, like the place kicker for the Forty-Niners, planted my foot squarely where it would do the most good. Pickering stumbled and went down. When he got up he almost ran to get away. I heard Gloria's front door slam. I followed and made sure the lock was securely set before I returned.

Just as I returned to Gloria's front room I heard the limousine's powerful motor start and the car pull away. I had a moment's pleasant vision of the lawyer nursing his broken nose. Then Gloria pointed out my own injuries.

"Peter, you're bleeding. It's not from the odious man's broken nose, either."

I held up my right arm and looked at it. A long, shallow scratch bled sluggishly. "It's nothing," I said. Then I saw that whatever had cut me had also ripped free the pocket with the key that had been delivered to my dressing room. It took me several seconds of hunting on hands and knees before I found it—and Roy Pickering's wristwatch. It must have come off in the struggle.

"I don't think I can mend this with needle and thread." Gloria said. She took Pickering's watch and saw the sharp edge where the wrist band fit into the watch bezel. "You'd think a successful lawyer would get something better than this. It looks like he picked it up at a secondhand store."

"He's a lawyer," I said. That pretty much explained any perversion or character flaw. I had met only a few whom I did not consider to be sociopaths, and all they talked about was getting into some other line of work.

"Please sit down, Peter. I don't know why you came by—or even how you found my house—but I'm glad you did. Can I get you something to drink? Coffee?"

"I don't drink coffee," I said. People always offer it, but I have an abiding hatred of the fierce liquid, including its unpleasant smell, which everyone always ohs and ahs over.

"Tea, then. I have some Darjeeling, I think."

"That would be fine." Gloria left to fix the tea while I made sure I was in one piece. Pickering's watch lay on the table. I just left it there, though I have to admit I was reaching for it when Gloria returned.

"I had the water already hot," she said, "when he came in. He just barged in. He didn't even have the decency to call first."

"What did he want?"

Gloria Gadsen sighed and sipped at her freshly brewed coffee. "He bought several of Taggart's paintings for Clarke Yancey. I didn't want to tell him but two of them were taken this afternoon. Pickering just wouldn't try to understand that I can't deliver what's been stolen."

"Didn't Yancey have the guts to come himself? Sending his pet lawyer is a coward's way of doing business."

"Yancey is an unpleasant person. I'd as soon not see him." Gloria shivered delicately. "I've told Marie that he is not to enter my gallery again. I know you felt I should have called the police, Peter, and what happened was unfortunate, but I had to make the most of the situation without a lot of fuss."

"He tried to rape Michelle."

"She's told you a little of her background," Gloria said. "With the money from the paintings Yancey bought I might be able to get her more help. She could never have testified against him. She's just not that strong yet."

"I find myself trying to protect her, too," I said. This triggered the memory of why I had come over. "She gave me your address because I need the guest list from Taggart's showing."

"The guest list? Whatever for?"

I told her about Jena Rosetti's murder, ending with, "I didn't tell Michelle because I didn't know how she would take it, what with everything she's been through in the past few days. Getting a job that puts her in the public eye and almost being raped is plenty for most people. Adding this . . .''

Gloria finished her coffee and leaned back in her wing chair, eyes closed and hands clutching the armrests. She was the vision of a woman too tired to go on.

"You do have the list?" I hated to push her, but I needed time to work out my own theories—and I was dog-tired, too.

When she moved it was in a single spastic motion that carried her across the room to a Chesterfield desk. She rummaged in a cubbyhole for a moment and then pulled out a much-folded sheet of plain paper and looked at it.

"Yes, Peter," she said after a few seconds. "I have it. I hope you can find whoever Jena was working for on it. I liked her. She came into the gallery regularly, always looking for work for her various clients."

I started to copy down the list when Gloria told me, "You don't have to return it. I'm sure Marie has a copy at the gallery."

I scanned the list, stopping only briefly on Clarke Yancey, Roy Pickering, and Jena Rosetti. The names were matched with addresses. Jena's I knew. The others might help. And there were another fifty names, many of whom I must have seen but didn't know by name.

"Thank you," I said. "Are you going to be all right? I don't think he'll come back, but I can call the police to send a patrol car around just to be on the safe side."

"He's off in a hole nursing his wounds," Gloria said. "I'll be fine. You take care of yourself, Peter. Roy Pickering—and Clarke Yancey—are not men to cross lightly."

"I can take care of myself," I said. "Do you want to keep his watch?"

"What? No, go on, take it. The next time you see that policeman friend of yours, give it to him for the Police Athletic League auction." She laughed at the suggestion of Pickering doing something for charity, even indirectly.

"Be sure all your doors and windows are locked," I said.

"You worry like an old woman. Now get out of here—scat. And be sure to let all the neighbors see you go. They'll think it's positively scandalous that I'm seeing a young man at this time of night."

I bent and kissed Gloria on the cheek, then left. I had Pickering's watch clutched in my hand. By the time I reached my car, I thought the watch was going to burn a hole in my hand. I slid into the BMW and put the watch down on the seat beside me. I knew I shouldn't do it, but I had to.

The trance was difficult to achieve. The level of relaxation needed was proving harder and harder for me—and along the way I had to consciously force away the jumble of other psychometric memories. The dead model's anklet. The penknife and the tie clip and the curiously soft feel from the key I had received tonight. More vague memories of sight and sound and odor swirled through my brain, taunting me, teasing me into trying just a little harder to separate them and make some sense from what I had experienced.

Even Magyar and Lady MacDowell and the bloody pentagram in my apartment rose to haunt me. I relaxed and finally erased the troubling thoughts. Tranquil, I floated and soared in the mist-world of my psychometric trance.

I picked up Roy Pickering's watch and almost screamed as the tangle of perceptions snake-danced through my head.

Blood exploded into my face. Howls of pain echoed in my eyes and I lived pain, intense pain being meted out. And I felt happy. More. I was on the verge of an orgasm. Pain and joy, joy and pain. They were inextricably linked.

The watch fell from my fingers and I pressed my sweating forehead into the cool plastic steering wheel.

I had seen more than I wanted. I had *felt* more than I wanted.

How was I ever going to put it all straight in my head and convey it to Willie Worthington?

CHAPTER 19

I sat and shook most of the night, staring at Roy Pickering's watch. I saw its vibrations, I *saw* more than just the visible. But I couldn't interpret what they really meant. There was blood and pain, and it wasn't Pickering's. He had done something terrible to someone else and had enjoyed it—enjoyed it in a sexual way.

Jena Rosetti kept coming to mind. Had Pickering had something to do with her death? He had been buying Taggart's paintings for Yancey at the gallery that night. Had she outbid him for her mysterious client?

I didn't have a good answer to that question.

I didn't have any answer to my question. The more I tried to concentrate on the problem, the worse it got for me. The pain from the earlier psychometrizing threatened to overpower me. I tried to keep it in check but my relaxation/trance techniques were failing. Needing rest but unable to take it, I wandered out onto my balcony and stared at the Golden Gate Bridge. The lovely structure spanned the distance to Marin County and Sausalito.

And it led to another world. Why I felt so hollow after Jena's death wasn't easily explained. The more I tried to analyze my feelings, the less clear everything became. The best I could say was that Jena had represented a hope, a potential, a possibility of a new future. I had seen something in her that I didn't see in other women. Her horrible death had also put a brutal end to my hope that we might hit it off.

I glanced back into my apartment at the watch lying on my coffee table. It might have been my imagination

or just the inundation of emotions from the psychometry but I felt that the watch's owner was guilty of a
heinous crime. The cold wind off the Bay helped blow
away my indecision. I went inside and called Willie
Worthington.

"So we've been thinking about Pickering, too. He's
never been one of my favorite people," Worthington
said.

"That's a hell of an understatement," said Burnside.
"After he got Yancey off on the racketeering charges,
you called him a—"

"I know what I said," Worthington cut in. He glared
at his partner. Burnside seemed not to notice he'd almost repeated something said in confidence after a
tough case. I remembered that Yancey had walked out
of the courtroom scot-free after Pickering had confused
the jury about the scope of the charges. In the SFPD
and the DA's office they still felt that the judge had done
nothing to clarify the situation.

"Forensics has the work-up on the hairs found on
Jena's body, don't they?"

"Yeah, so? We can't use them as evidence unless we
can tie them into somebody. We'd need a damned near
airtight case for that."

"Red hair," I said. "Roy Pickering's chauffeur is
redheaded."

"So's a quarter of the men out in that squad room.
So we got a bunch of micks? That's not proof. We can't
just arrest his guy because he's got red hair."

I stared at the watch. Roy Pickering was guilty of
something. I just couldn't be sure what.

"We're bringing him in," Worthington said unexpectedly. "We're going to sweat him a bit."

"There's no percentage in that," I said. "He's a lawyer. He knows he doesn't have to say a word."

"We might get him to cut a deal," said Burnside.
"We might be able to lay things at Yancey's feet and
implicate him."

I almost laughed at this. Burnside knew better. Anything Yancey told his lawyer was privileged information. Pinning anything on the pair of them would be doubly hard—maybe four times as hard. So long as the two men hung together they'd never hand separately. And both had had enough experience with the law to know it. There just wasn't enough evidence.

"Burnie's got the details wrong, but the main idea's okay," said Worthington. "Pickering will never cop to anything, but we can home in on him and start the fires burning. We might even be able to get Yancey to cut him loose."

"Too much notoriety?"

"Something like that, Peter. And we might know a bit more about this than you do." Worthington looked up. A uniformed officer was motioning to him. "There's our guest of honor now. Let's let him stew for a few minutes in the interrogation room."

"He knows the tricks," I said.

"The reason we use them is that they work on most people," Worthington said. "There's a need to confess or at least to brag. Pickering is a lawyer. He likes to win. Who's to know he's done anything good unless he tells us, huh?"

Worthington heaved himself to his feet and motioned for me to come along. I picked up the watch and slid it into my new jacket's pocket. I'd taken the time to do a little shopping before I drove to the Hall of Justice, so I was somewhat more presentable than I had been. I'd have to buy an entire wardrobe sometime if I wanted to replace everything that had been destroyed when my apartment was trashed.

"So good of you to come, Mr. Pickering." Worthington pulled a chair around and sat in it.

"Am I under arrest? The officer who brought me in wasn't clear on the subject. I haven't been read my rights."

"No fooling," Worthington said. "It's hard to imagine that a lawyer doesn't know and understand his rights in today's world, especially a sharp trial lawyer like you.''

Pickering sat and stared ahead, saying nothing.

I placed his wristwatch on the table. He looked up. He didn't seem to have noticed me before. His nose was a mess and would require considerable cosmetic surgery to get it back into shape. Since the lawyer had probably had a hand in Jena's murder, it bothered me that the broken nose was likely to be the only punishment he got.

''So you found it, Thorne?'' He slid the watch onto his arm as if nothing had happened between us. If he wasn't going to press the point, neither was I. Gloria would never bring charges against him if there was an outside chance he would continue to buy high-ticket artwork from her gallery. She ought to put her foot down, but the lure of big bucks was too much for some people.

In a bout between money and principles, money usually won two falls to a submission.

''Tell us about your client, Clarke Yancey.''

''I represent him. We have a privileged attorney-client relationship. More than this I'm not at liberty to say.''

''You buy paintings for him, don't you?'' asked Worthington. The detective seemed almost sleepy, but I knew he was alert and watching Pickering's every twitch. What the lawyer might reveal wouldn't be admissible in court but it could give Worthington a new avenue for ferreting out other information.

''I do. That's public knowledge.''

''You also have a conflict of interest with Yancey, don't you?'' Worthington leaned forward. I hadn't been paying too much attention to the line of questioning until now. Where Worthington was headed was beyond me.

''I don't understand.'' The beads of sweat on the lawyer's forehead told me that he understood all too well. I hoped Worthington would let me in on this.

"You hire people to go out and bid on paintings, then you sorta jack up the price to Yancey. Or maybe you like the same stuff he does. You couldn't buy it without him getting upset, so you send out people to do the buying for you."

"I have hired art experts from time to time," Pickering said cautiously. "That isn't a crime. It certainly isn't a conflict of interest."

"That's right," said Burnside, "it's no crime, it'd just be between you and your boss. But Yancey might like to know you hired Jena Rosetti to do some buying for you."

"Prove it," the lawyer snapped.

"Not too hard to do," said Worthington. "We've got her records. We've even got a tape recording of the two of you discussing how to screw Yancey over on a bid. I don't think she knew what was going on, but that's what happened. She outbid you at an auction, then you went and 'bought' it from her afterward for Yancey at a big markup. I doubt you and she split the difference, did you?"

Roy Pickering said nothing, but he was sweating hard now. I smiled. This was going better than I'd've thought possible. Worthington was telling the lawyer he might just spill the beans to Clarke Yancey about how he had been taken—how many times? For how much? Something told me the quantity of either wouldn't matter as much as the feeling of betrayal.

People who betrayed Clarke Yancey ended up floating facedown in the Bay.

"Did Yancey find out?" I asked aloud. "And did you tell him Jena was the one who double-crossed him? Were you the one who set her up to be beaten to death?"

Worthington glared at me. I bit my lip. I had no place asking that. In a manner of speaking, I was just along for the ride, an interested bystander but not an active participant. The way the detective built his case was important—but so was pinning the crime on Roy Pickering. I *knew* he had something to do with it. The psychometry on his watch showed that he had done more than kill someone. He had killed with fervor.

The son of a bitch had enjoyed it.

"What is this, a Star Chamber? I don't want to say anymore," Pickering said. He slumped in the chair, his arms crossed and his legs tight together, the perfect picture of body language telling everyone the conversation was over.

For Roy Pickering it might have been, but Worthington was just getting started.

"Look, I know how it is," Worthington said. "She was a pretty broad, but dumb, you know? You didn't mean to do more than scare her. It wasn't your fault she upped and died on you."

I thought Worthington had gone crazy. He was telling Pickering it was all right that he had killed Jena. A cold look from Burnside told me to keep my mouth shut.

"I didn't have anything to do with that," the lawyer said. "But she did double-cross me and I didn't like that."

"I know how it is," Worthington said sympathetically. "You can't control the men who work for you. They get a little excited sometimes. They do things you might not want them to do, but in this case she still had it coming. Leastwise, that's what I think."

Again Burnside's glare kept me quiet. To my surprise Roy Pickering almost confessed.

"I only wanted to teach her a lesson," he said.

"And it got out of hand," Worthington finished for him. "That driver of yours, he was the one who did the beating, wasn't he?"

Pickering nodded slightly. "Break her legs was all he was supposed to do."

"He just got carried away," Worthington said. "Burnie, get the counselor a cup of coffee. I've got to do some work in the office. Keep him company for a while, okay?"

Worthington's partner nodded curtly. Worthington left the room after putting a reassuring hand on Roy Pick-

ering's shoulder and smiling. I trailed him, madder than
hell.

"Willie, how can you—"

"Can it, Peter," he said tiredly. "I got as much out
of him as I'm likely to. He won't come out and confess,
but he might just as well have. Now we have enough
to pin the Rosetti killing on him."

"You were telling him it was all right to do what he
did!" I was outraged.

"So? What I say doesn't have any legal bearing. I'd
agree with him that the world was flat if it would pry
loose a confession. That doesn't make the world flat,
does it?"

"But—" I was almost sputtering. Worthington went
into his cubbyhole and punched a number on the phone.
"Lab? Get a sample of hair from the perp Burnside is
holding in interrogation room four. See if it matches
with the black strand we got in the Rosetti case. Yeah,
thanks. Sure, we'll have a match for you on the red hair
soon enough."

He hung up. "That's the way it's done. Pickering
gave us enough to believe we can get the court order to
check his driver's hair. He's a bully boy from your description, a leg breaker. This is the way I figure it. Jena
Rosetti was working for Pickering. When she got
burned with the forgery he wanted to teach her a lesson."

"He had his driver break her legs?"

Worthington nodded. "The guy got carried away or,
if the autopsy report's right, a blood clot formed and
she died of a stroke. I wouldn't be at all surprised if
the driver went berserk and did the head damage then."

"It was Pickering," I said. "He beat her and *enjoyed*
it."

"Oh, yeah, the watch. But you said you couldn't be
sure it was Rosetti he was getting off on hitting."

"It had to be her." I felt numb inside.

"Probably was. We'll sweat the driver and see if we

can't nail both their hides to the wall. If we have to, we'll let the driver cop a plea and nail Pickering for this one. He hasn't been popular around here for a long time.''

Worthington sat down heavily in his chair. A smile slowly crossed his face, then he laughed.

''What's so funny?''

''Maybe justice can be served by letting Pickering turn state's evidence against the driver. And then we let Yancey know his own mouthpiece was screwing him on the art purchases. If we watch carefully enough, we might be able to nail Yancey for his lawyer's murder. Yeah, I like that.''

Too much had happened too quickly for me to appreciate the finer points. It hardly seemed over—and it wasn't by many months of hassling in the courts—but Jena's murderers were in custody, or soon to be, and good cases could be made.

''Don't be so down in the mouth, Peter,'' the detective said. ''Even if we don't get Yancey this time, he'll fall sometime. He's into too many crooked things not to.''

I thrust my hands into my pockets. My fingers rubbed over the key that had been delivered to my dressing room. I pulled it out and looked at it.

''What's that?'' Worthington craned his neck to see what I was staring at so intently. I might have been looking at the key but I wasn't really seeing it.

''I told you about the penknife and the tie clip. This is a key someone left at my dressing-room door last night. I don't get much off it.''

''You mean when you psychometrize? It sounds as if someone's just yanking your chain.''

''The only things stolen from my apartment were the penknife and the tie clip,'' I reminded him. ''Someone wanted me to look at them, then stole them back.''

''Any progress on the break-in?'' he asked me.

''Nothing,'' I said.

"Why don't you leave the key and let me do some poking around?"

I shrugged. The key wasn't important. I handed it over and left, still fighting the barrenness of losing Jena.

CHAPTER 20

I hardly knew what I was doing most of the day. Everything kept spinning around in my head, keeping me off balance and more than a little confused. I finally managed to replenish my wardrobe, but the sales clerks must have thought I was on drugs.

I wish I had been.

Taking Willie Worthington at his word did little to ease my mind concerning Jena's death. I knew the DA's office was sincere in wanting to put Roy Pickering behind bars. It was as much a personal vendetta with the prosecutor as it was a legal matter. And even if they cut Pickering a deal to testify against his driver in Jena's murder, the lawyer was still in hot water with Yancey. Worthington's idea of letting Clarke Yancey know what his lawyer had been up to demonstrated a certain cynical sense of justice.

It might not be a formal constitutional justice but the proper end would be served.

What really troubled me were the other odd things that had begun intruding into my life. Even aside from the psychometric images from the half-'n'-half murders, I was unsettled by the knife, tie clip, and key. The undercurrent in the three items made me apprehensive. What made it worth breaking into my apartment to steal two of them back—and then giving me the key the next day?

Someone was toying with me, but psychometric readings from the three articles gave me no hint about who or why. They told of apprehension, some pain, some surprise, but what was the real cause of it all? I had no idea.

I returned to my apartment to find workmen busily repairing the worst of the damage. A plumber grumbled and growled constantly as he removed the pipes on my bathroom sink and replaced them with new lengths of PVC.

"If you try puttin' that shit down these babies," he told me, "the whole fuckin' pipe will fuckin' dissolve. You understand what I'm saying?"

I didn't bother telling him I'd had nothing to do with clogging the pipes. He went to work on the drain in the bathtub, this time swearing constantly. These pipes weren't as accessible as the ones under the sinks. I left him to his work and went to check on the painter. He stood and stared at the wall where the bloody pentagram had been sketched.

He shook his head and went back to work.

"What's wrong?" I asked. "You aren't satisfied?"

"Can't get the pattern covered," he said. "I'm using top-of-the-line paint and there's still show-through. A couple extra coats might work, but I'll have to let this dry and come back. Can't work it into my schedule until next week if I do that. You mind?"

I stood and critically studied the man's handiwork. He was right about the paint not covering the pentagram. "What makes it stand out like this?"

"Whoever did it knew what he was doing," the painter said. "He used just the right amount of vermilion acrylic mixed in with the blood. Damned near impossible to remove without having to replaster the wall, and you can see how hard it is to cover up."

"It wasn't just blood?"

"I've seen about everything," the painter confided. He used broad brush strokes across the wall in a vain attempt to hide the fierce red star. "I used to work for the city. Painted out graffiti. Now *that* was a thankless job."

"You came across graffiti done in blood?"

"Goat's blood, sometimes. Those Satanic punks think it's funny. Other times the cops told me it was pig blood. The gangs'd break into a butcher store or somewhere like that and steal gallons of the damned stuff, then slather it all around. I got good at recognizing it—even figured out ways of getting it off stone and concrete." He sniffed in contempt. "No defacement was better'n me and my paint. But this?"

"Real hard stuff to get off," I said, coaxing him along.

"Somebody who knew what he was doing did this. No street punk is going to take the time to mix this up. Hell, most of them can't even read the instructions on the tubes of glue they sniff." He stepped back and shrugged. "This is the best I can do until it dries. I'll give you a ring next week to let you know when I can get back to it. Lemme leave my paint out on your balcony. No need lugging it around."

The heavy paint smell was giving me a headache. I dragged my day's shopping into the bedroom and began hanging up my new clothes. Shopping isn't something I enjoy, and I'd wasted most of the day trying to get enough to carry me through a week without forcing me to wear my stage costumes.

I shed the jacket I was wearing and laid it out. Remembering Michelle Ferris, I tried to call and arrange for a rehearsal later in the afternoon. Her phone rang a dozen times before I gave up.

Yawning, I sat down on the bed intending to just rest for a moment. The plumber swore as he worked. The rattle of his pipe wrench and other tools came to me. A soft breeze came through the bedroom window and cleared away some of the pungent paint fumes. The bed seemed more comfortable than I remembered. I lay back and stared at the ceiling, my eyes chasing dots around.

Relaxation stalked me and held me in its gentle grip. My eyelids drooped. Without meaning to, I fell asleep. When I awoke it was almost 6:30. I jumped from bed, trying to rub the sleep from my eyes. I blundered into the bathroom, intending to take a shower. The plumber had left the pipes in the bathtub exposed. Where the water would have gone if I'd turned on the shower was beyond me. The people in the apartment below probably would have been upset at the miniature flood coming down on them. I had to content myself with just washing my face.

It was for the best, anyway. I was late and had to get to the Rialto. Michelle would be beside herself if I didn't show up to reassure her before we went on. For a new assistant, she was getting damned little rehearsal time—it was all onstage experience. She was a quick study, though, and the performances had gone as well as could be expected. The only problems had been mine and not hers.

I changed and tried to figure out some way to convince her of this. She had about the lowest self-esteem I'd seen in a long time.

I got to the theater a little after 7:15 and went directly to my dressing room. Forty-five minutes to prepare for a magic act is little enough, but to my surprise Michelle hadn't arrived yet.

"Have you seen my assistant?" I asked the lighting director.

The man pushed out his lower lip, looked thoughtful, and finally said that he hadn't seen her since yesterday.

Thanking him, I made a quick circuit behind the stage looking for her. None of the stagehands had seen her either.

"What's the matter, Thorne?" asked Barry Morgan. The theater manager sat on a crate, his hands folded behind his greasy head. "You lost another one? That babe was too good lookin' to last long with you. She had class."

"Michelle didn't even call me," I said. I tried to remember if I had left on the answering machine. If I had, there might have been a message from her I hadn't noticed.

"So you going on without her? You only got twenty minutes before the curtain."

"I can't do the act without an assistant," I said irritably. My mind raced. No easy answers came. Michelle wasn't like Julianne or a few other assistants I'd had over the years. She might not have a good self-image but she was dependable. Whether this came from a need to please me or from a decent set of values concerning other people's time was something I had no idea about. But I believed she was reliable.

I went to the pay phone and dialed Gloria Gadsen at her home. She answered on the second ring.

"Gloria, Peter Thorne. I'm looking for Michelle. She should have been at the theater an hour ago."

"Why, that's odd," Gloria said. "She came in to the gallery this afternoon around three-fifteen. She had to wait while I settled accounts with Taggart. He kept trying to persuade me to have another showing of his work, but frankly this one has been far too trying an experience for me to consider it anytime soon. When he left, and he was *very* unpleasant, as usual, Michelle and I had a cup of coffee and talked for a while."

"How long?"

"Not that long, Peter. It couldn't have been more than twenty minutes. She left a little before four. I remember because Marie's watch battery had died on her, and she kept asking me what time it was."

"Michelle left before four?" She should have reached the Rialto with time to spare.

"You don't think there's something wrong, do you? Should I call the police?"

"No, that's all right. She might have gotten tied up in traffic." Bits and pieces refused to fall together right in my mind. It was as if I stared at the pieces from half a dozen jigsaw puzzles all mixed and laid on the table. Not only did I have to piece them together, they all had to go into the proper picture.

"Gloria, wait, before you hang up, what can you tell me about Taggart?"

"What?"

"Taggart, the painter. What can you tell me about him? His background, his family, that sort of thing."

"Why do you ask, Peter?"

I didn't have a good idea why I was asking and admitted as much to her. "There's something to be said for playing a hunch."

"Do you think he's done something to her because I wouldn't agree to a new showing? Why, that good-for-nothing ingrate. I'll string him up by his thumbs if—"

"What about his family, Gloria?" The clock was ticking. I had less than fifteen minutes before curtain. Unless Michelle Ferris walked in now, I wasn't going on.

Gloria Gadsen laughed harshly. "They are all as freaky as he is. I met his brother, but I can't recall his name. He works for some Scottish company that thinks they can open a chain of haggis restaurants in the U.S. You know what *that* is, don't you?"

"Sheep's stomach stuffed with entrails," I said, distracted. "That's his only family?" I didn't know what I was angling for. Some berserk restaurateur was not it.

"Oh, there was his sister. I don't remember her name either. She fancied herself a psychic and did crystal ball readings. She'd been arrested on fraud charges several times."

"Lady MacDowell," I said in a low voice. The resemblance between brother and sister was obvious now that I thought about it.

"Yes," cried Gloria, "that was her name. Or stage name, actually. I heard something happened to her. She probably got sent to prison."

"She committed suicide," I said.

"You knew her, then?"

The cold knot in my belly grew until it was larger and sharper-edged than the iceberg that had sunk the *Titanic*. I didn't know what was going on, but Taggart—and his dead sister—figured in it.

"What's Taggart's address?"

"You mean where he lives? I don't know. He's never there, anyway. I'd call and call but he was always out. He's got a North Beach studio where he works, but there's no telephone listed for him there. Taggart isn't the type of man to have an unlisted phone number." Gloria snorted in disgust. "He probably wanted his name in twenty-point bold in the phone book so nobody would miss it."

"The North Beach address'll do," I said. North. North of Worthington's office. North, north, north. Panic rose within me and threatened to seize control. I forced myself to stay calm outwardly but inside I was turning into an electric pudding that quivered and sizzled. This was worse than the coldness it replaced.

"Hey, Thorne, five minutes to curtain," bellowed Morgan from the wings. "We got an okay house tonight. Do good and I might extend you for a week. Fuck up and you're done. I won't even let you come back for tomorrow's show. Got a good animal act waiting to try out. You got that?"

I put my hand over the telephone and called to Morgan, "So cancel me. Right now."

The manager sputtered and stormed over. I didn't have time for him. "Gloria, the address. What is it?"

"Here it is." She gave it to me. I hung up before Morgan tried to slam me against the wall. Sidestepping his crude attack, I ducked past him and ran to the dressing room for my car keys. I left by the side exit, Morgan screaming at me the entire way.

My career was important, and I'd never walked out like this just before a performance, but my gut feeling was that Michelle Ferris's life was in danger. If I didn't do something fast, Taggart just might exact revenge for his sister's suicide.

North. Something about the direction kept slicing at my brain. North, north, North Beach.

CHAPTER 21

I drove like a madman until it crossed my mind that I couldn't do anything alone. I had to notify the police. For all the ads the companies run, finding a pay telephone was almost impossible. A small Chinese grocery had one precariously hanging on its north wall. I double-parked and jumped out, hoping that the phone worked. When I dropped my quarter in, a satisfying dial tone came back. I quickly punched in Worthington's number.

"Sergeant Worthington," came the almost immediate response. He must have been at his desk working late. I thought about that for a moment and tried to figure out if he ever went home. For all his complaining about his wife's cooking, Worthington must put away a lot of it on his off hours. Even the high-fat-content hot dogs and other fast foods he stuffed into his mouth didn't account for his bulk.

"Willie, this is Thorne. Michelle Ferris didn't show up for the eight o'clock show."

"You told me she was a basket case. That's too bad. Did you cancel?"

"That's not important. I talked to her aunt, Gloria Gadsen. She said this afternoon Michelle left the gallery a few minutes after one of Gloria's artists. The only name I have on him is Taggart. His sister was Lady MacDowell, the one who blew herself up."

"Oh, yeah, I remember that. It wasn't my case but everyone in the squad room was buzzing about it. You yanked her chain and she went off the deep end, right?"

"Taggart might be trying to get revenge on Gloria

for not giving him another show or he might be aiming to get back at me for his sister's death. Or he might think kidnapping Michelle is a great way to get both of us.''

"Whoa, wait, Peter. You're getting ahead of yourself. There's no proof this Taggart has anything to do with Michelle Ferris. Everything you said about her tells me she's what we love to call an 'unstable personality.' She might have decided to see if the grunion were running down in Venice and just took off. Or who knows what could have entered her head?''

"It's not like that, Willie. Believe me. He's got her and—''

I stopped. The words jumbled in my throat as I strained to get my thoughts in order. The concepts were clear in my head but something scrambled them before I could speak. The wild dancing swirls and the prior psychometry on the items passed me during my performances—and the key I'd given Worthington—everything. It all tied together but the chaos raging in my head prevented me from telling the detective what was happening.

"If you say so, Peter. She might just be out on a date, you know? But I'm glad you phoned. I was going to call you later.''

"Why?'' I had to convince him this was important. Sweat poured down my face and soaked my shirt.

It hurts! Don't do this to me! My skin! You're skinning me alive!

I put my head against the cold grocery wall and listened to Worthington as I tried to find the right words to persuade him of the danger facing Michelle.

"That key you gave us was very interesting. It turned out to belong to Marcie Comstock.''

"Her apartment? In Marin?''

"Are you all right, Peter? You sound weird. Somebody got a gun stuck in your ribs?''

"My apartment,'' I whispered. Blood flowed in rivers down my chest and pain rose within me, starting in my legs and creeping upward until it reached my waist.

Suffer! Suffer like I have! Suffer and create!

"Not your apartment, Peter, Marcie Comstock's. That's who belonged to the key. How did you get the key?"

"I told you. It was outside my dressing-room door. Left by the same man who passed me the penknife and the tie clip. Why?"

"You're asking my questions," Worthington said. "Come on in to my office and let's talk this over."

"Michelle," I said. Pictures flashed before my eyes, all remnants of the psychometry I had done earlier. All tied together in ways I couldn't understand. It was all the same and it was all directed at me. I was the nexus for pain and suffering and hatred, and I had to stop him.

Taggart. I had to stop him from hurting Michelle as he had done the others.

"There have been six," I said.

"What are you saying? Peter, I'll send a car for you. Where are you calling from? I hear traffic in the background. You're not in your apartment."

"Taggart's killed four others just as he did Marcie Comstock and Westman."

"Who's Westman?"

"The man. The second half-'n'-half, the man with the belt buckle. The man who owned the penknife and the tie clip. Taggart was taunting me, but I couldn't reach the right level to see. Too much else blotted my vision. He took the knife and the tie clip before he began his torture. I got only hints of what Westman must have experienced. Too much of Taggart came through. It was like watching a movie through a gauze curtain—or alternating reels of two movies. And the key. He must have taken it from the model before he began torturing her. Willie, you can't believe the suffering she went through. The agony!" I was becoming hysterical and couldn't control myself.

There wasn't an immediate response. A series of

clicks sounded. Worthington was tracing the call. Even through an electronically switched exchange, tracing a call takes several minutes.

"I'm going to his studio, Willie. He's got Michelle and I have to stop him before he harms her."

"Wait, Peter, hold on. Give me the address."

He was trying to stall me. He thought I had gone around the bend. And I had. The sensations that had been so disjointed before snapped into a coherent picture now. The pieces I had thought that belonged to several pictures were all from just one.

Taggart.

Please, rape me, do what you want but don't do that again! No, not upside-down. I don't want to die!

I sank to my knees as the impact of the psychometry hit me over and over like storm waves crashing against the eroding coastline. The stark pain and fear. It was almost more than I could bear. But I got no sense this was what Taggart sought. He wasn't like Roy Pickering, who got a sexual thrill from beating up women. The lawyer might have even climaxed when he struck Jena Rosetti and knew she was dead. I hadn't been able to get all the details from his wristwatch, but the emotion of hate and pleasure was so powerful it lingered. Killing Jena probably wasn't his first excursion into those dark realms.

But Taggart? Revenge, possibly, but what else? What of the model and Westman and the other four? There was an uncontrollable temper, but that didn't come into play. Not exactly. It did and it didn't.

I began to cry in frustration. It was all so clear—and all so clouded.

"I don't know who they are, Willie," I sobbed. "Their pain is a shadow, a ghost fluttering through my mind. It's added to that from Comstock and Westman, an echo of their passing and no more. But I don't know who they are."

"We'll be there in a few minutes, Peter," he said, trying to soothe me.

"His studio," I said stiffening with resolve as I rose above the pain from the others. "I'll meet you there." I gave him the North Beach address and then hung up.

I hadn't realized that I had been putting on a small psychodrama performance for the neighborhood kids. Several of them stood nearby, just watching. They ranged in age from fourteen to early twenties, all Chinese and all impassive but obviously interested in eavesdropping on my conversation.

I raced for my car and roared off. Whether Willie arrived before me or not wasn't important. Stopping Taggart was the overriding necessity.

And I wasn't even sure he was at his studio, though the part of me in touch with the resonances from the psychometric readings *knew*. He was there and he was going to make Michelle his seventh victim.

In San Francisco cable cars always have the right of way. I brushed against one and got the gripman's savage invective and the passengers' obscene gestures as I careened down California Street. I darted in and out of traffic and only good reflexes kept me from being in several crashes.

I drove into the North Beach section, a century and more ago the heart of the city. Now it was filled with hulking warehouses and wall-to-wall housing filled with would-be artists and others who think it's trendy to live here. Just looking around at the grinding poverty everywhere depressed me even more.

I began cursing as I drove up and down the unknown streets as I hunted for Taggart's studio. When I realized that I had driven by it three times, I was even more furious with myself. Seconds mattered. What was going on I couldn't say, but he had to have kidnapped Michelle. Nothing else fit into the psychic matrix that formed so violently in my mind.

The warehouse was immense, covering almost the entire city block. Finding anyone inside would be the work of a company of men. I drove back and forth on a side street hunting for any sign that Taggart was inside. The brick exterior was a modern-day castle resisting all attempts at storming. I got out and checked every door I saw. Each was securely fastened. Even if I decided to drive through the door, I wasn't convinced I could break down the steel-plated behemoths. It was as if Taggart had purposely chosen this place for its security.

Tiring of getting out and climbing back into my car after checking five different doors, I finally parked and decided the only way to gain entry was to take the high road. The locked doors weren't just fastened with mechanical locks—they had drop bars behind them. There are ways of getting past such security measures, and I know most of them, but they might take an hour or longer. I didn't have the time.

Searching for a good way to climb to the roof brought me to the eastern side of the building. I had just started my hunt when I saw the white van. It was the one that had almost run me down just before I'd discovered Gloria Gadsen's gallery had been burgled.

As cautiously as I could, I went to the van and peered inside. The darkness gave me no chance to see what might be carried in the rear. I placed my hand against the stubby front that served as a hood. The engine was still warm, but not so hot that I could imagine Taggart had just arrived. I tried to decide how long ago he had kidnapped Michelle. Hours. An engine might cool down this much in two or three hours.

If Taggart had done anything at all to Michelle . . . I closed my eyes and tried to put more order into the enervating chaos whirling around in my head. Facts meant nothing; everything I believed about Taggart was derived from my psychic power. It wasn't logical, it wouldn't stand up in court, and it was probably wrong.

But it wasn't wrong. I *knew* it was right. Taggart was a serial killer, a mutilator and a particular fiend unlike anyone I'd ever come across before.

Circling the van convinced me that it had been here for some time. Wet spray from the Bay had soaked it but the pavement beneath was dry. I gingerly tugged at the rear door handles. To my surprise the van wasn't locked. The doors came open.

For several seconds I wasn't sure what I was looking at. My stomach churned and tumbled and I almost lost everything I had eaten. My vivid imagination made it seem that I was staring at human bodies partially covered with canvas tarpaulins. As my eyes adjusted to the lower level of light inside the van, I saw that what had appeared to be a body was nothing more than a stack of frames.

I jumped into the rear of the van and began pulling away the tarps. It was as I had suspected when I'd seen the van. Taggart had robbed Gloria's gallery of his own paintings. I flipped through them as if I were rippling a deck of cards. After I finished, I went back and did it again. Something was missing from the stack; several paintings I knew to have been stolen weren't here. I heaved a deep sigh. Taggart had stolen back his own work and had already found buyers for some of it. What I didn't understand was why he hadn't taken all the paintings. Why only steal some of the collection on display in the gallery?

And why hadn't he simply told Gloria he was retracting the offer to sell? The stolen paintings had no bearing on their sold or unsold status, according to Gloria.

I started to duck-walk out of the van when I saw another painting. This one had been wedged between the van's exterior wall and the inner struts so it wouldn't roll around. I tugged hard and got it free.

Maelstrom of Disquiet was as disturbing a piece now as it had been when I'd first seen it displayed. Jena had commented on its power, and even Jason the art critic had been taken by it. Studying the bold strokes and vibrant colors didn't give me any clue why the piece gave me the shudders.

My hands rested on either side of the painting, on the rough-hewn wood frame. At first I thought I had brushed off some glue. My fingers felt sticky. I looked at them and my hands were as clean as they could be after trying to open so many doors on a filthy warehouse. On impulse, I placed my hand flat on the center of the painting, as I had almost done when it was in the gallery. When Taggart had shouted at me and stopped me from making physical contact.

Now something more hit me like a sledgehammer.

. . . killing me! The pain. You're skinning me alive. Stop, stop! Why are you doing this?

The surge of torment rocked me back. My hands remained on the painting, as if stuck there. The psychometric vibrations increased and forced themselves onto my senses. The usual jumbling didn't occur this time. The floodgates of potent emotions opened and let stark agony wash over my senses.

Skin. It's leaving my arm. And the prop blade. It's spinning. No, don't do this, the pain, I'm bleeding, why are you putting me into the propeller, the steel edges cut, cut, CUT!

Blood gushed from my lower torso. I slammed back against the other side of the van, causing the vehicle to rock on its springs. It came as a huge revelation that my legs were still fastened to my body. I—Marcie—had been lowered headfirst into a spinning propeller and slowly turned into hamburger. It had taken me—Marcie—long minutes to die as the blade had slowly worked it way up, to my wrists, to my elbows, and then to my shoulders.

Anguish! My arms were snipped off and the pain drove me wild.

I fainted. Before I struggled back to the state of fearful consciousness the time might have stretched into minutes. I doubted I had been out for more than a half hour. Again, I checked my arms to reassure myself that they were still whole.

Taggart had fed the woman into a whirling prop and slowly cut her to ribbons.

Other psychometric remnants returned to haunt me. Scissors. I had gotten flashes of scissors snipping when

I had touched the tie clip passed to me during a performance. Westman's tie clip. The second body Worthington had dragged from the Bay. He had been murdered just like Marcie Comstock, one slow, excruciating inch at a time.

I stared at the painting and wondered why it carried such power with it. Usually only metallic objects have the resonant capacity to store such psychic energy. Something had locked the woman's travails into the painting.

I wished I had never met Michelle Ferris or Gloria Gadsen or had Worthington call me in on the half-'n'-half murders. My mental condition deteriorated. I couldn't keep thinking straight. The deaths intruded more and more—and the screams of agony! They filled my ears, and rivers of red blinded me; I smelled the coppery scent of blood.

More blood than there was in the world inundated me, drowned me, and made me crazy.

I exploded from the van, unable even to look at *Maelstrom of Disquiet*. On hands and knees, I crawled to the edge of the building and leaned against its secure bulk. Cold crept up my back but I ignored it. The desolation within was worse than anything the night air could do to my body.

"Michelle," I muttered, focusing on her to give me purpose and to drive away the madness engulfing me. Her image came to my mind. Like a man seeing a life jacket, I clung to the vision. She was in danger. I had to help her. If I didn't, she would die like Marcie Comstock and Westman and four others. She would die horribly, hideously, in a bloody fountain.

My mind could never become totally numbed to the horror of Taggart's crime, but I achieved both purpose and a measure of self-control as I rose up to stand. I had experienced death—Marcie Comstock's death. Sweat poured down my body in spite of the chill night. I hardly noticed. A transformation had occurred. I had become a knight on a sacred mission. Rescue Michelle Ferris. That was all I kept lodged firmly in my head.

I set off to find a way into the warehouse to rescue her. I made one complete trip around without finding anything better than a rickety ladder on the side of the structure. Rusty iron fire escapes rose to the top of the four-story building. Climbing on top of a dumpster, I balanced on shaky legs and then jumped, wrapping my fingers around the bottom rung of the escape. To my surprise the ladder didn't slide down under my weight. I swung back and forth, got a better grip, and then curled myself backward and kicked myself out flat on my belly onto the fire escape. I made my way up the ladder, checking each window as I went.

They were not only secured with iron bars set into concrete, someone had nailed heavy sheets of three-quarter-inch plywood to the inside of the windows. It would take both a hacksaw and a battering ram to get into the building this way. Dynamite might be even better.

I kept climbing. It was all I could do. When I got to the roof, I checked the streets to see if there were any red or blue flashing lights. A part of me died when I saw nothing to indicate that Worthington had sent a couple prowl cars my direction.

Pain, piercing pain, rocketing up my arms and into my head. Don't kill me, please, don't do this!

I was shaken to the core of my being. I could no longer hold the psychometric images back. They imposed themselves on me. Marcie did. Westman did. Laura and three others did, their fear and pain and suffering becoming mine. I closed my eyes and shook all over. Somehow I was getting more and more psychometric information, and I wasn't even in contact with anything owned by the victims. It was as if their tortured souls were reaching out to me, imploring me to stop Taggart before he killed again.

Blood blinding me, flying up, splashing everywhere,

getting into my eyes—and the rising tide of pain! I'm dying and it's a relief. There can't be any more pain in the world. I've used it all up and the blood, always the blood!

I took another look out across the city. I saw red flashing lights, but they were in the distance and going away from the area. This wasn't what I wanted to find. I needed help. And I wasn't going to get it from the police.

Whatever happened would be between Taggart and me. Worthington might have not believed me, I might have failed to communicate how sure I was that Taggart was responsible—I don't know what had happened. Maybe he thought I had gone insane. The patrol cars might even have been diverted to some other more immediate crime. Worthington was always complaining about his staff being taken for routine drug busts that were puffed into front-page stories.

I turned from the building's verge and started across the roof. I hadn't gone ten paces when I noticed how difficult it was to walk. The roof was sticky with tar. Here and there were fresh patches. I found a bucket filled with the gooey black stuff and wondered if this was the source of the asphalt dumped down my drains. If it was, Taggart hadn't needed to go far to get it.

The roof was a dark and ominous expanse that promised little—until I saw the pale yellow gleam through a skylight. Running on cat's feet, I got to the edge of the skylight and peered down. The dirt on the window made seeing difficult. I rubbed a patch clear with my sleeve and pressed my eye against the chicken-wire-laced glass.

It took several seconds for me to decipher what I saw. Taggart had appropriated the entire loading bay of the warehouse for his studio. He must have had ten thousand square feet, and most of it was used for storage of enormous marble and bronze pieces. They were bizarre sculptures, disturbing mythic, nightmarish creatures cavorting, fornicating, doing terrible, perverse things to one another. I knew how Dante had felt when he first glimpsed Hell.

There was a difference. Dante was able to describe it, to put it into words. I couldn't even force the words to rise into my paralyzed brain.

I shifted position so I wouldn't have to look at the monstrosities Taggart had fashioned from beautiful material. What I saw was even more horrifying.

CHAPTER 22

I couldn't hear Michelle screaming, but I knew she was. She had been fastened, naked, so that she dangled several feet above the concrete floor. Her hands had been chained together and the chain hung over the hook of a crane. Moving around and cleaning a bit more of the grime off the window, I saw Taggart standing at the crane's controls. He jerked her up by slow inches. But that wasn't what made my heart almost explode in my chest.

He was raising her so that he could move a large airplane propeller under her. All I could do was watch in utter fascination, just as a moral person witnessing a bear baiting or a cock fight is caught up in the hideous sight. It was terrible and yet there was a grisly fascination to it that prevented me from moving away. Averting my eyes was even less possible than movement. I *had* to watch the horrific scene unfolding beneath me.

Michelle began swinging to and fro on the chain, obviously pleading with Taggart. The man's expression was partially hidden, but he didn't seem to be gloating. It was almost as if he had just gone to a nine-to-five job and was experiencing a few minor, but not entirely unforeseen, difficulties before getting down to serious work.

Taggart cranked her up to almost ten feet off the floor before stopping. Michelle twisted slowly so that every few seconds I saw the expression of stark, unrelenting fear on her face. I tried to think what she must be feeling, naked and vulnerable—and about to be dropped feet first into a huge fan blade.

I tried and couldn't imagine the terror.

The sweat pouring off my face was what brought me out of the trance Taggart had put me in. In some way I knew now what a bird experiences when faced by a snake. The sweat ran into my eyes and blurred my vision before dripping onto the window. This further obscured my view. The double action made it possible for me to push away and get a grip on myself.

It almost wasn't possible. The remnants of my earlier psychometries rushed back to disorient me. The sight of Michelle, Taggart, the propeller blade, and the studio had released the hidden torrents that I had sensed earlier and had somehow managed to file in some sort of psychic memory.

He's a killer! The pain! Make him stop torturing me!

Another voice rose inside my mind. I couldn't tell if it was male or female. *Please, I can't take any more. Stop him. Stop him and free me from the agony! My legs are being sliced off!*

And another and another joined the mental din. They sounded like a Greek chorus in my head. I thought my brain would rupture under their urgings—and the memories of their anguish.

I rolled over and over on the roof, getting sticky from the tar patching. I came to my hands and knees and knew I couldn't just let Taggart kill Michelle Ferris. I had to stop him. But how? The only door I saw on the roof was securely fastened. Going to it, I checked the way the hinges hung on the door and knew it was almost impossible to get through this way. The door was locked and probably barred on the inside, and the hinges were likewise out of my reach. Circling the small wood structure, I finally saw how I could get in.

A plank had warped and allowed me to peer through. More than this, I was able to get my fingers between the boards. Bracing my feet, I heaved. I don't have great muscle bulk; I'm not a weight lifter. But I need both a wiry power and agility for my escapes, when I do that kind of act. All my strength and skill at getting free of various seemingly impenetrable containers was now reversed. I used all I had learned over a lifetime to force my way into the building.

The warped wood began giving way. The nails came free with a sudden ripping noise louder than any gunshot. I didn't worry that Taggart might have heard this. He had seemed too intent on feeding Michelle into the rotary meat grinder to come see what was happening on his roof, even if he had heard. The first board was like the first domino in a long row. It fell and the others followed quickly. I wormed through the small opening I'd made and tumbled down the narrow stairs toward the main floor of the old warehouse.

A rat's maze spread out around me. I had expected to find the main room quickly. A series of hallways and locked doors worse than any psychologist's experiment confounded me. I picked the lock on the first two doors, but this took so much time I knew it wouldn't do. I had to move faster. I had to get to Michelle and stop Taggart. Panic rose but I forced it away. This wasn't the time to let myself get frantic.

And it proved harder than ever. I was worried about Michelle, but the psychometric voices were coming clearer. It was hard to tell what was my own thought and what rose from the trapped resonances of Taggart's victims.

With some deliberation, I found a door marked EXIT. The panic bar gave way but the door opened only a few inches. A chain secured it on the far side. But through the gap I saw Michelle's naked body swinging back and forth. It gleamed with a sheen of fear-sweat. She was kicking in a vain attempt to stay above the whirling blade of Taggart's death machine. The artist moved around, muttering to himself and totally ignoring her.

This made no sense to me. A madman was supposed to lord it over his victims, enjoy their struggles, even get perverse pleasure from their fear. Roy Pickering's wristwatch carried a grim reminder of that.

The disgust I felt for this rose within me and blocked off the cries from Taggart's victims. Along with this moment of silence came the first respite I'd had from their remembered suffering. I reached through the gap between door and jamb and found the chain holding the door shut. The lock was a simple one. Pulling it to me, I got it around to where I could see it. The picklock and my skill proved too much for it. The hasp slid open within seconds.

I hoped I had worked quickly enough on the lock. I kicked the door open and burst into the warehouse, feeling like a frustrated movie superhero. Michelle still struggled at the end of the long chain, drawing her legs up to keep her feet from the blade. Of Taggart there wasn't a trace.

Running to her, I called out, "I'll turn it off. Hang in there." The inanity of the pun escaped her and did nothing to bolster my own spirits. Fear is the great destroyer. I was being killed along with Michelle, inch by slow inch. All she had to do was die. I had to watch it happen.

And if I did, I'd relive it a million times. The voices crying in my head assure me of that fate.

"Where's the switch?"

"Peter, behind you!" Michelle swung in a huge arc; this only saved her from imminent danger at the extremes. She couldn't keep it up much longer. Some diabolical mechanism was lowering her into the spinning propeller just as the swinging blade had come down on the poor wight in "The Pit and the Pendulum."

I thought she was telling where the switch was. I turned and saw a huge fist exploding into my face. I jerked to the side and let Taggart's knuckles glide along the side of my face. The blow glanced off my cheekbone but still stunned me. I stumbled back and fell, too dazed to keep my balance.

"You meddling son of a bitch!" he roared. "You're never satisfied. You killed my sister. Now you're trying to fuck up my work. I'm not going to let you!"

"Taggart . . ." The name slipped from my lips. I focused my eyes and saw him hefting an iron rod. He swung the long, heavy bar with contemptuous ease. The man's power was immense.

"I never much liked my sister. She was a fool. But she was my only kin and you drove her to suicide."

I rolled as the bar crashed into the concrete where I had lain an instant earlier. I kept rolling and came to my feet, searching for a weapon of my own.

"Why are you doing this?" Would he look toward Michelle for a split second and let me rush him? No. His eyes stayed on me as he answered.

"Art, you fool. I'm doing it for art! What else is there in this fucked up world? Models are for helping with the process of creation."

The iron shaft almost tore me in half. I tried dodging and almost made it. The bar crashed into my ribs and pain unlike any I had ever known exploded inside me.

Worse! It gets worse! The pain!

The echoes of my psychometry came to me now. Those Taggart had already killed had endured this and more. Somehow, rather than disheartening me, it gave me the will to fight him. He had broken a rib and smashed something important inside my chest. I felt the liquid gushing within, but I still had some fight in me.

I was in good shape, but Taggart fought harder, aided by the demons locked inside him. His wild-eyed countenance told me I could never best him by trying to fight. And running was out of the question.

"You're going to die, Thorne. You made my sister want to die and you tried to stop me from creating my artwork. None of you understand me. You laugh at my work because you can't understand it."

"Why'd you take your own paintings?" I tried to get

him onto another tack. Distracting Taggart looked like the only way I might stay alive for a few more seconds.

"She was *giving* the best ones away! I wanted them for my own collection. Hell, I'd sooner destroy them than let them go to people who can't appreciate my genius."

Over Taggart's shoulder I saw Michelle doubling into a tight ball, her legs pulled up to her chest. This gave her another two feet of clearance, but the mechanism continued lowering her. She couldn't keep this strained position for long; even if she could, the lengthening chain would drop her into the spinning propeller. Her struggles would only add to the splattering of her blood, just what Taggart sought.

"Why are you doing this to Michelle? Is it because of me? Because of her aunt?"

"What?" This took Taggart aback. He hesitated. It gave me the chance to dart back, down a small corridor formed by piles of packing crates. "That's not it. God, you're an incredible idiot. You don't understand art and you don't understand me!"

"You trashed my apartment," I called to him, stumbling back along the narrow passageway formed by the wood crates. "Was it to get back the knife and tie clip?"

"Of course it was," he said. Spittle ran down his chin. The fire in his eyes was enough to fry eggs. His hands shook with eagerness to slaughter me. "I've heard about you. You claim you can touch an object and see into the life of its owner. My sister had a gift and you killed her because you were jealous. I wanted to test you with her death. You failed!"

And I would die soon. The pain in my side doubled every second. Curtains of red alternated with black. I was going to pass out. The voices in my skull grew weaker and weaker. My own senses were fading, too. I leaned against one of the crates and followed it to the floor when it slipped off the stack.

"You're pathetic. You know nothing about art—and

you don't know shit about psychic powers!'' Taggart rose above me like Nemesis. I kicked feebly and connected with his kneecap. He howled in pain. It only takes twenty psi to break a kneecap, but my ineffective kick hadn't done more than bruise him.

I crawled back the way I had come. As long as I stayed between the crates he couldn't swing the iron rod in a wide arc. But he could raise it over his head and bring it down on me—and he did.

New pain erupted like a volcano as it crashed into my spine. I was driven flat onto the concrete floor. Sure that he had broken my back, I wiggled forward. I crawled back to the area where we had first collided and saw that Michelle was almost lost. She was sobbing hysterically and the blade whipped past just under her, missing her by scant inches.

Painfully, I got to my feet and knew there was no way in hell I could ever stop the blade in time. I turned as Taggart rushed me. The iron rod missed crushing my skull like an eggshell—and I attacked. Using every last ounce of energy locked in my body, I drove forward. My arms circled Taggart's thick body. I caught him up in a bear hug that was horribly weak.

But I didn't intend to crush the life from him with my arms. I used the momentum of his rush and twisted, lifting as I went. His feet came off the ground—and his head rose up through the death-dealing circle of the aircraft propeller blade.

The last thing I remembered before I blacked out was the red rain falling as warm and gentle as the first spring drizzle against my face.

CHAPTER 23

Bright lights flashed in my face. I turned from them but they followed like heat-seeking missiles intent on driving their warheads into the deepest recesses of my brain. Rolling over, I pressed my face down into my hands, wondering what was going on. There was a curious emptiness inside that I couldn't immediately identify.

Then it came to me. The psychometric remnants of those Taggart had murdered were gone. The echoes in my skull were at last silenced. This made me wonder if I had died. Trying to recreate what had happened proved futile. The more I thought, the less clear I became on my condition—or Michelle Ferris's.

"Michelle!" I tried to sit up and found I couldn't, not lying on my belly. I tried to roll back but the furor around me swallowed me whole. In the far distance I heard voices I almost recognized. "Michelle," I said, weaker.

"She's fine, Peter," came the voice of God. "You saved her."

"Taggart."

God spoke again. "He's dead. From what Michelle told us, you picked him up and threw him into the propeller. Parts of his skull got caught in the bearings and the blade seized up. A good thing, too, since Michelle said she wasn't able to hang on much longer."

"Yeah, and that was quite a sight," came another voice. "She's damned good looking naked. I know why he chose her, but it was going to be a hell of a waste of a good piece of ass."

"Shut up, Burnie," came God's voice.

I struggled to come to hands and knees, thinking I might crawl off and explore Heaven. Somewhere in the midst of this physical exertion it came to me that God sounded suspiciously like Willie Worthington. I lifted my head and saw him and his partner a few feet away.

"Willie?"

"Welcome back to the real world."

"Shit, he was just communing with the spirits," said Burnside. "You know how it is with these psychic bozos."

"Burnie, go play in the traffic. I'm sure there's something you can do somewhere else that you won't fuck up too badly." Worthington sent his partner away. I finally came into a sitting position.

"What happened?" I asked inanely. "I don't remember much." The world had a curious flatness to it, as if some demented artist had removed the dimension of depth. Even the colors were muted and different, somehow paler and less intense. I wondered if my experiences had burned out something in my brain.

"The doc looked you over and patched your ribs. He gave you a feel-good shot so you're probably not feeling much pain. As to Michelle, she's off to the hospital for a checkup and then to her aunt's place for a little R-and-R. She's had a rocky time of it, but she seemed in good enough spirits."

The muzziness around the edges of my mind suggested Worthington was right about the painkiller. Nothing much bothered to me; I drifted in a limbo of pain. I knew I was in pain, but it just didn't matter.

"She's not a stable personality," I said. "She's been through more than just this. She needs a shrink."

"Michelle's all right," he said. "We got in just a few minutes after you tossed Taggart into his fan. She was about the only coherent one around at the time. You ought to have heard my squad fall to pieces when they saw this set-up and what clogged its bearings. Damnation." Worthington turned and stared at the contraption. "We've been going over this place with a fine-toothed comb. We can definitely pin four murders on him. The guy must have been completely whacko. He kept mementos from each crime, recorded everything in a notebook, and even took photos. Shit."

I remembered how detached Taggart had been. This wasn't a crime in the usual vein. He had been an artist at work. A sociopath, yes, but still an artist.

"Look at the way he had those canvases pulled around where her blood would have splashed," Worthington said. "You have any idea why he was feeding his victims through the fan blade like that?"

"Air brushing," I said.

"What?" Worthington looked at me as if my head had fallen off and rolled along the floor. It could have and I'd never have missed it. The painkiller was working wonders on me. I ran my fingers along the thick tape on my ribs and twisted slightly, feeling the bandages taped along my spine.

"Rembrandt," I said, striving to keep my thoughts in order. "The old masters used different colors of paint to keep others from counterfeiting their work. And one of them—I can't remember who—used ground up gold and precious gems."

"Vermeer," Worthington muttered.

"So Taggart used human blood." The full realization swept over me and made me dizzy. If I hadn't been sitting tailor-fashion on the floor I'd've keeled over. As it was, I wobbled from side to side.

"He mixed blood into his paint? So why did he feed them through a propeller to get it?"

"Nonobjectivist art," I said. "The blood spattered in different patterns as the victim struggled and died. Then Taggart went back and air-brushed his own designs around the basic pattern left by the flying drops of blood. I've heard of some artists just throwing paint into the wash from a jet engine and letting that splatter their canvas. Taggart was a little more imaginative."

"That's sick," Worthington said, but there was a hint

of admiration in his voice. "He got pictures no one else could duplicate and he didn't even have to do much work. Slide his victim down into the blade, let them turn to hamburger and then use what was left as art."

"Six victims?" I asked, remembering the psychometric voices.

"We've got four identified. There might be a couple more. We'll know when forensics finishes. And you were right about one being named Westman. And Marcie Comstock was there in his notes. He took a lot of pictures of her, before and after." I'd never seen Worthington turn white before. He did now just mentioning the photos. I knew I never wanted to see the pictures or know what the young model had looked like as Taggart worked on her. She must have taken a freelance modeling job with him and gotten far more than she had bargained for.

"He stole his own pictures from the Gadsen Gallery," I said. "He said he didn't want Gloria selling them to people who didn't know his true genius. If you find the pictures, you'll see that they're all the ones he did using human blood."

"We've got forensics doing blood typing on the pictures," Worthington said. "We might be able to match everything up." He shrugged. "It doesn't matter. You finished him off for us. It's just as well. This would have been a media circus if we'd taken it to trial."

I swallowed hard. My mouth was dry, and it wasn't just from the drugs the doctor had injected.

"He would have sold millions of dollars worth of paintings," I said. "The public . . ."

"They're assholes. All of them," Worthington said.

"He was the one who trashed my apartment," I said. I remembered now that my Japanese woodcuts hadn't been destroyed. The artist in Taggart had been too strong to destroy such beauty. But he hadn't liked my lobby posters of the old magicians. All that remained of them was colored confetti.

"Yeah, I wanted to ask you about that. You said something about his sister."

I didn't remember that, but then I hadn't been totally conscious—and I still wasn't in good shape.

"Lady MacDowell," I said. "She was his sister. Apparently he helped her kill herself, and he blamed me for it."

"There wasn't any question it was suicide. I looked over the file after you called."

"Check the entire warehouse," I said. "There might be some paintings he did using her blood."

Worthington flipped through his notebook, got out his pencil and began chewing on it. I let him think for several seconds before asking, "Well? What about it?"

"We found some canvases that were shredded as if a knife had slashed them. We thought it was just a case of the artist getting bent out of shape over something he didn't like and reacting badly. There was a considerable amount of reddish brown splotching on the canvases. We'll check it out and see if it's blood, too."

I sat and stared at the rig Taggart had put around his canvases. The large one on the floor would have caught most of Michelle's flying blood as her body entered the prop and its heavy steel blade flung off gore in all directions. The tall canvases on stretchers forming loose-fitting walls on three sides would have been hit with trickles that would run down them in random paths. Taggart could have made four complete paintings from Michelle's bloody death. He was improving on his own techniques.

And he would have taken the remaining half body and thrown it into the Bay, as he had done before with Comstock and Westman. The only difference would have been which half remained. Michelle would have been recognizable. I wondered about the others Taggart had killed. Top or bottom half through the grinder?

I almost broke down and cried that such a grisly question could have occurred to me.

"We're checking everything out," Worthington said. "There's a pier not fifty yards from here. It wouldn't take much to bring a boat in and take the body out into the Bay."

"He might have just tossed the bodies off the pier," I said. "He was done with them." The sheer aloofness from humanity this implied chilled my soul. To Taggart art was the entire universe. The only vibrant paintings he did were those using another life force. He wasn't as much an artist as a vampire. The taunts he had used on Westman were only to make the man struggle; Westman must have been one seriously deranged man to need such goading.

"We'll get it all wrapped up, Peter. Why don't we get you on home so you can rest?"

"Why didn't you come down here right away?" I demanded, suddenly furious at Worthington. "I told you what I knew. The psychometry . . ."

"Yeah, well, we were real busy. Roy Pickering was spilling his guts to us about all manner of things. He pinned Jena Rosetti's death on his driver, but he kept on talking so much that we think the DA can indict Yancey again. With Pickering as our star witness, we might even send him up for a few years."

"But Pickering is as guilty as his driver. He was the one who ordered him to beat up Jena for buying the forgery."

"You know it and I know it. We might even be able to get a jury to believe it, but the DA sees bigger fish swimming in the pond."

"Clarke Yancey." I was suddenly more than tired. I was exhausted and needed to sleep for a week.

"You know how it is. But Pickering's the kind of scum bucket who'll make a big mistake on his own. We'll nab him then."

Worthington helped me to my feet. I tried not to look

back but I did anyway. It might have been my imagination but I thought I heard faint screams of pain.

The psychometric memories endured.

It was going to be a long time before they faded into the white noise of my brain.

JAMES ELLROY

"Echoes the Best of Wambaugh"
New York Sunday News

BROWN'S REQUIEM   **78741-5/$3.95 US $4.95 Can**
Join ex-cop and sometimes P.I. Fritz Brown beneath the
golden glitter of Tinsel Town...where arson, pay-offs, and
porn are all part of the game.

CLANDESTINE   **81141-3/$3.95 US/$4.95 Can**
Nominated for an Edgar Award for Best Original Paperback
Mystery Novel. A compelling thriller about an ambitious
L.A. patrolman caught up in the sex and sleaze of smog city
where murder is the dark side of love.

KILLER ON THE ROAD   **89934-5/$4.50 US/$5.50 Can**
Enter the horrifying world of a killer whose bloody trail of
carnage baffles police from coast to coast and whose only
pleasure is to kill...and kill again.

Featuring Lloyd Hopkins

BLOOD ON THE MOON   **69851-X/$3.95 US/$4.95 Can**
Lloyd Hopkins is an L.A. cop. Hard, driven, brilliant, he's
the man they call in when a murder case looks bad.

BECAUSE THE NIGHT   **70063-8/$3.95 US/$4.95 Can**
Detective Sergeant Lloyd Hopkins had a hunch that there
was a connection between three bloody bodies and one
missing cop...a hunch that would take him to the dark heart
of madness...and beyond.